BEFRIENDED

THEO KEVIN MAGEE

Published in the United States of America

Brilliant Books Literary
137 Forest Park Lane Thomasville
North Carolina 27360 USA

ISBN:
Paperback: 979-8-88945-231-7
E-book: 979-8-88945-232-4
Hardback: 979-8-88945-233-1

CONTENTS

CHAPTER 1

THE BEGINNING OF THE END

The arguing in the kitchen continues to grow louder as the guest in the dining area hear Julia and Grant arguing over the meal. The guests seem to be in shock that this quarrel is taking place—only one room away from them.

"NO, Julia! NO! That's not the way these are supposed to be made!"

"Grant, I have been cooking for longer than you have been eating! Will you let me finish my dish, then we'll let our friends decide if it was properly prepared."

"I can tell you right now that you won't like the response that they'll give."

"You know, Grant, sometimes you are unbelievable, stinking unbelievable!"

Grant storms out of the kitchen. Slamming his hand into the swinging kitchen door and walks straight up to his room. Carol gets up from the dinner table to go check on Julia.

When Carol walks into the kitchen, she sees Julia with her face buried in her hands, crying uncontrollably.

"Julia? Are you okay, sweetie?"

"Yeah," Julia wipes her eyes. "Yeah, I'm fine. I just need to find the oregano. I know I bought a new bottle." She talks while still crying.

"Julia, I know it's none of my business, but why do you put yourself through this?"

"You're right Carol. It is none of your business. If you're not here to help me find the oregano, can you please leave me be."

"I was only trying to help." Carol runs out of the kitchen and back to the dinner table to gather her things.

"Where you going, baby? What's wrong?" Now Carol is crying.

"We're leaving, Tim."

"We just got here, and I'm hungry."

"Well we can stop at Burger King on the way home."

"But … but …," says Tim.

"But nothing! You either leave with me or walk home." Tim stands up and tells the remaining four guests to have a goodnight, and it was nice to meet them.

As they are exiting the door, Grant comes downstairs out of his room and walks right behind them.

"Hey, Grant?" says Tim. "I thought you were not feeling good or something."

"Nah," says Grant.

"Where you headed, Grant?"

"To get me something to eat."

"Ain't Julia in there cooking for you and some people?"

"I guess, but I don't want that. It's not gonna turn out right."

"How do you know? You haven't even—," Carol cut in.

"Well, you take care Grant, and take care of Julia for me too."

Grant keeps walking without saying a word as he enters his car and leaves.

Julia figures that Grant has already left, like he always tends to do after a heated battle of words.

So she musters up her pride, goes into the dining room to tell her guest that she is horribly sorry, and that she is going to postpone this get-together. Julia has tears in her eyes, and the guests began to embrace her one by one before they leave.

Now, all alone, she cuts off the stove and fixes herself a sandwich. She sits in the dining room by herself, waiting for Grant's return.

A few miles away, this young, single dancing choreographer is wrapping up a session with his people in a downtown studio. Jake walks over to his personal items and grabs his water bottle. As he drinks, one of his female dancers comes over to him and starts to make conversation with him. It's obvious that she is trying to flirt, but at this particular time, Jake's interest is not in her. Jake is a player. Jake travels from city to city and town to town. He's even been out of the country a couple of times due to the nature of his career. He's been hired to teach dance techniques to a variety of people, groups, or individuals. That's why he loves his job. But one thing he loves more is the thrill of the chase. As Joyce keeps talking, Jake nonchalantly asks her if she can excuse him for one minute. He then places his drink back into his gym bag and walks over to a group of his dancers. One female dancer stands out to Jake the most, and that is the one he targets. From that moment on, it is all about the thrill. The chase has begun. After some cunning words and some humorous statements, Jake has her commit to a date later this evening. Jake walks away a champion in his sport. He is now about to go home and prepare for his night out.

As he reaches his car door, he notices that he has several missed calls on his phone. Some are business-related, but most of them are past flings, as he would call it. Right when he hangs up his cell, it begins to ring. It is Samantha. He is kind of reluctant about taking the call. Jake doesn't have it in his plans to listen to nagging the whole night, but before the cell stops ringing, he answers it.

"Hey, Jake!"

"Hello, Samantha."

"So did you get the message I left you on your phone?"

"Well, I just got out of rehearsal. I didn't check any messages yet, but I will. Why? Are you okay?"

"Yeah, Jake, I'm fine. I just really need to talk to you face to face."

"We can't talk over the phone?"

"I really don't want to; but I need to say what needs to be said." Samantha takes a deep breath then releases. "Jake, I don't know what I am to you, but I can't be that anymore. I know you are fine with us being what we are, but it's killing me." Jake tries to jump in.

"Wait, I thought—"

"Just let me finish, please, Jake. I can't do this, maybe one day you will find your soul mate. Obviously, it's not me. It seems like I'm just your soul mate between the hours of 1:00 a.m. until 4:00 a.m."

"You are right, Samantha. I'm sorry. Maybe one day I will find my mate out there, I won't hurt you no more. I won't call you, e-mail you, facebook you, or any of that. If you want to get in contact with me, you know how to find me."

As Samantha continues to cry, she thanks Jake for his understanding. Then Samantha hangs up the phone. Jake stands with the phone to his ear for a minute, then he takes it down and looks at Samantha's contact information. He is just about to delete it, then he says to himself, "Nah." And closes the phone and continues with his plans for the evening.

Now back at the Richards home, Julia is fast asleep on the couch downstairs when Grant comes home. He quietly gets ready for bed himself. Instead of going into his room in his nice bed, he takes the covers off the bed and curls up with Julia on the couch. She feels his presence, scoots closer to him, and smiles as she sleeps.

This pattern in their relationship happens more than it doesn't. It is just now starting to wear down heavily on Julia. After three years of marriage, she thinks she could continue to take it, turns out she isn't built for this much drama.

Julia works as a receptionist for a medical clinic in the heart of the city. On most days, she brings her home troubles to work with her. She is good at covering them up to clients and most co-workers. Grant, on the other hand, is an electrical technician. He cannot hide his feelings from anyone. Nor can he hide his love and faithfulness toward his wife.

As Tim and Grant are working on a project in a high-rise, Tim says to Grant. "Did you check out that hot blonde in the last cubicle?"

"Nah, I'm too old for her, she would just use me for all my money. Then she would just blow it on weed for her boyfriend." They both laugh. "Besides, I gotta good thing in Julia. I just—," right then Tim cuts in.

"I know you need to get it together. How long have you guys been married?

"Three years, closer to four."

"Then why do you still have angry spells the way you do, especially toward her?"

"I don't know. I guess I'm just built in a different way. I mean look at you. You have your faults too. I haven't seen you walk on any water lately, Tim."

"True, true, but we're not talking about me though, Grant. We're talking about you."

"Who brought me up? Weren't we talking about the blonde in the last cubicle?"

Tim laughs. "Yeah."

"I would rather talk about her than mention your name." They both laugh and continue to work and talk.

(Back at the dance Studio)

During the middle of a dance rehearsal, the tour director comes to talk to Jake.

"Excuse me everyone! Excuse me!" Everyone stops dancing as the music stops.

"Jake, can I have a word with you for a minute?" Jake pauses with a look of concern on his face. "Sure, I'll be there in a second."

Jake walks into Danny's office and closes the door.

"Ah … Jake … Jake … Jake."

"What?" Danny pauses in silence. "What ... What ... What?" Jake says.

"We did it, buddy!"

"We did what, Danny?"

"We grew a fan base."

This puzzles Jake. "We already have a fan base. Are you telling me that it's now larger?"

"Jake, didn't I just say that. Never mind. Look, in a month, we are going back overseas. Our show is in demand."

"It is!" Jake says excitedly.

"I'm not just talking about one show. I'm talking many!"

"How many, Danny?"

"I'm talking about pack-your-bags-for-two-to-three-years many!"

"Wow! Hold on, Danny. I can't up and leave for that long. That's what this talk is about?"

"Would this amount of earned income convince you to go?" Danny shows him a contract with a six-figure salary plus a bonus. Jake sits down in the chair, shocked.

Jake stands up and walks to the door. He turns to Danny and says, "Do you have a pen?"

Danny pulls out a pen. Jake goes over the contract and the time length of the work. He leaves Danny's office in delight.

As Jake is walking back to the studio, he glances out the window and sees Julia walking toward her work building with a coffee cup and some documents. He watches her until she walks into the building and out of his sight. He thinks to himself, This is it, my last fling in the States. I bet we are going to have fun together. Jake continues to walk down the hall to tell the dancers the good news.

Julia now begins to situate herself behind her desk. She is happy today because she is only working half a day. She and Grant are given tickets to the opera. She looks at this as another chance to reconnect with Grant.

When Julia counts down to the last thirty minutes of her day, she calls Grant to see if he is ready for tonight's big event. Grant responds back to her.

"Big event? What big event?"

Julia laughs and says to him, "The opera, silly."

"Oh, um, I forgot about that. Uh, I'm just go come out and say it. I'm not in the mood for an opera. I'm not feeling opera-ish right this instant.

"Grant, so when will you be feeling opera-ish? We've had these tickets for a week, you told me that if they were free you would go! Grant, these are free and you're still not going!"

"Not really."

"Not really what, Grant?"

"I'm not really going. Let's just sit home and stream a movie from Netflix and —"

Julia cuts in, "You can do that by yourself!" Julia hangs up the phone.

Grant takes the phone away from his ear and stares at it and says to himself, "I told you I wasn't going."

As Julia tries to compose herself within her work area, she calls her boss's phone line and tells the boss that her plans are cancelled. The boss responds back with, "So are you saying you can work your full shift?"

"Yes, I can, Monica. I can work my whole shift."

"Thank you, Julia! I would have been so lost without you."

"No prob, Monica," Julia says with a sad voice.

"Are you okay, Julia? I hope you didn't cancel your plans just to help me?"

"Noooo! Don't be crazy. Some other plans came up that my husband didn't inform me about, so it just works out better to cancel and reschedule."

"How rude and stubborn of him not to mention these plans! I hope they're worth him sleeping on the couch tonight."

"Yea, they are Monica. Yeah, they are."

"Okay, let me get back to work then. Mr. Trudale cancelled his appointment by the way."

"Oh, okay good. That's one less old sack I have to fondle."

Julia says, "Ewwww!" as they both laugh. Then they both hang up and continue to work.

When five o'clock hits at the dance studio, Jake tells his exhausted performers to call it a day. As tired as Jake is, he doesn't forget about the lady in the building he seen earlier. Jake goes into the restroom, freshens up himself a little, then grabs his gym bag, and heads for the door. He crosses the street to get to the medical building. As he glaze through the buildings glass doors, he sees a women approaching the doors. Jake attempts to open the doors, but just as he began to pull on them, Julia twists the lock on them.

"We're closed, sorry."

Jake is speaking through the doors.

"I'm not here to get a checkup or anything, I just wanted—"

Julia chimes in again. "You can come back tomorrow at 9:00 a.m. We're closed."

"No, no I just—" Jake looks at her face and notices the cold hard stare she is giving him.

"Okay, I guess I'll come back tomorrow. What time—"

Julia jumps in. "Nine. That sums it up then. See you tomorrow," Julia gives a cold smirk. Then she turns and walks away from the doors.

Jake shakes his head and says, "This just might be harder than it seems."

That night when Julia finally makes it home, Grant is watching a movie on Netflix in the bedroom. Julia goes over to the side of the bed he is lying on and stands over him. She quickly snatches her pillow from underneath his head and says,

"This is mine!" Then she storms out of the room.

"Hey! Where you going?"

Sarcastically answering, Julia yells out, "To the opera!"

She then grabs an extra blanket out of the hall and heads downstairs to the couch.

The following morning is business as usual, as everyone reports to work. Jake is definitely going to introduce himself to Julia this time. He just wants this impression to be better than his first.

The day progresses into midday, and Jake gives the order for everyone to take a break. He tells everyone to rest for an hour, and then report back to the studio. Jake on the other hand is about to go pay the medical clinic a visit. With no direct plan in mind, he's about to just wing it. Besides, that's how he gets his best results.

When Jake steps into the facility, it is nicely cooled by the air conditioning with soft music playing in the background. There are a few clients waiting to be seen. Nothing out of the ordinary is happening in that office at this time. Jake continues to glance around the office. As he approaches the receptionist desk, that's when he spots Julia. Her back is turned toward Jake. She is checking over some files on the back wall. Jake doesn't get nervous; he just springs right into game mode. He clears his throat to get her attention. Julia turns around and looks at Jake like she's seen him before. Julia greets him and asks him how she may be of service.

"Well," Jake says, "is this where you would come to get a physical?"

"Why? Yes, it is."

"How long has he been a practicing doctor?"

"Ms. Reeves has been a board-certified doctor for a little over twenty years now."

"If you would just look over my right shoulder you'll see all of her credentials. Now, Mr.—?"

"My name is Jake McKhal."

"Mr. McKhal, take these forms and fill them out please, and make sure you sign them."

"Okay, will do Miss—," he pauses for her name.

"Oh, my name? You can call me receptionist or secretary. Either will do."

"Wow. It's like that?"

"The chairs are right behind you, Mr. McKhal."

Jake then turns around and heads for the seats. In his mind, he thinks that this will be a tough match, but it's not a lost cause. Dr. Reeves comes out to talk to Julia about a client rescheduling, and she observes Jake sitting in the waiting room filling out paperwork. "If you have to bump a couple of clients to get that man in my office before five, then do so." Julia looks at Dr. Reeves and laughs as she comments on Dr. Reeves comment. Jake glances at Julia as she laughs and thinks to himself, "So she does smile."

Jake receives the earliest appointment as possible. Julia calls him to the front desk and points to the room he is taking his exam in. Julia says to him,

"Room number 3 on the left. Have a good day, Mr. McKhal." Jake then enters the room and began his checkup from Dr. Reeves. While Jake is getting his checkup, he throws in a couple of questions about Julia in their conversation. Dr. Reeves answers the question, not knowing she is helping Jake accomplish his goal.

As Jake leaves the office, he passes the receptionist desk and says, "Bye Julia. I'll see you around."

Julia looks up surprised that he knows her name. She gives Jake a grin and says, "You to, Mr. McKhal."

The following day, Jake arrives at the doctor's office thirty minutes before closing. It is practically empty in there and Julia is busy entering information into the computer. Jake approaches her desk holding his stomach and moaning. Julia looks up and asks out of concern,

"Mr. McKhal, are you okay?"

"No, I'm sick."

"What's wrong? Never mind. Let me go and get Dr. Reeves."

"No, no. Ever since I have seen your smile yesterday, it's been making me sick to my stomach that I didn't leave here with your number." He gives one more good moan.

"Mr. McKhal, you scared me. I was beggining to think something is seriously wrong with you! Then you break out with that corny line. How may I help you, Mr. McKhal?" Jake straightens up.

"You can start by calling me, Jake."

"I don't get formal with patients."

"I'm not your patient. Dr. Reeves is my doctor."

"Mr. McKhal, I hav—,"

Jake jumps in. "Okay, okay, I get it. You just struck me as someone who could have become my best friend."

"Mr. McKhal, how old are you?"

"I'm twenty-seven years old."

"Well, I'm older than that and my husband is also my age. I'm too old to play games."

"So now you're telling me you are married."

"My relationship is my business."

"Would you like to share with me?" Jake says.

Julia smiles a little bit and says, "No, I would not. Listen, Jake you sound like a nice guy but this is one bet you aren't winning."

"Bet? What bet?

"I know you got a buddy that put money on us hooking up, but it isn't happening."

"There's no bet, no buddy. Just me, just you," says Jake.

"Look, I have to get back to work."

"Okay, Ms. Julia. Just remember one thing."

"What's that?"

"You called me, Jake. You're getting formal with me already." Jake does a little dance move and he spins in the direction of the door and leaves out in joy. Julia looks at him as he leaves, shakes her head, and starts to grin. Then Julia continues to work.

The next business day comes and goes with no sign of Jake in sight. Now Julia isn't into him, but she does like the attention Jake gives her. Everything continues to flow smoothly throughout the day. It ends as peacefully as it starts. Julia arrives home later in the evening ready to wind down. She is expecting Grant to beat her home this night, but he gets held up at the bar with Tim. It isn't until two hours has gone by that Julia finally hears keys rattling in the door.

"Good evening, Mr. Richards, how was your long night?"

"It was good. Tim had an issue at home with Carol and he wanted to talk it over with me."

"Where did you and Tim end up going?

"To Odools."

"O'Dools, huh?"

"You don't even drink, Grant. Don't you think of all people I would know that."

"I had a milk on the rocks. Tim was the one getting floored."

"Okay, if you say so."

"See what I mean, Julia, what is that comment for? Do I reek of alcohol or something? Am I stumbling as I walk? I mean, come on! My friend needed me, and I was there. These are the kinds of issues that occur when you have friends. You should try and get you some."

"Did you just really go there, Grant? You should have been the one getting wasted and spewing your guts about your relationship, not Tim!"

"We don't have issues. I don't have an issue, maybe it's all in your head," says Grant.

Julia starts to tear up. "Why is it never: 'Hello, honey. How was your day, honey. Let me rub your back, baby—.' It's always this between us!"

"What? What's this?"

"This is friction. Friction, Grant! We're like oil and water. I don't see why—," Julia stops talking.

"See why and what, Julia? Come on Julia, you're a big girl. Spit it out! You don't see why we're still married? You know what? Me neither!"

After Grant says this, he turns toward the door and leaves back out. All Julia hears is the car starting up and the car pulling out of the driveway. Julia then sits on the couch. She grabs herself a blanket, and cries herself to sleep.

Julia wakes up the next morning feeling a little down and out, but nonetheless, she's re-energized. She starts her daily routine to get ready to go to work. She goes into the bedroom and notices the bed was unmade, so Grant was there. Julia thinks to herself. She takes a shower and dresses herself. Julia then gets ready to head out the door. She heads into the kitchen to grab herself a cup of coffee and there lies a dozen roses on the kitchen table. There is no note, but of course, she knows who they are from. Julia bends over to smell the roses then she grins at the notion. She steps out of the house and begins her commute to work.

Julia's day seems to be going so-so. She hasn't gotten cursed out, spilled her coffee, or gotten yelled at by her boss. It's a couple of minutes pass 2:00 p.m., and Julia is expecting these next hours to go by smoothly with no delay.

Something outside of Julia's medical clinic is attracting the attention of her clients. She decides to look out the window to see what is going on herself. It seems to be a group of people in some type of formation lining up outside. It is all confusing to her until music starts playing. The group of twenty people start to put on a show. The group is not just drawing the attention of the clinic, but of passerbyers as well. Julia begins to giggle as she sees who is leading this group. Through all of the dance steps, Jake is peering through the clinic to see if he sees Julia. For a split-second, They lock eyes. Jake winks and goes into the finale. The dancers rock that street. They receive applause and whistles from the crowd. After a minute or so, the dancers all make their way back to the studio, as did Jake. Julia sits back down at her desk and continues her work.

For the better part of the two and a half hours, all she thinks about is the show outside the window. She wonders is it for her. Julia decides that after work, she is going to the studio to ask Jake that very question.

With the work day complete, Julia finishes up her daily close out reports and locks up the office. She then heads to the dance studio, where Jake and the group has one more performance going on. Julia stands there and watches Jake and his team work. She's impressed by their moves, especially Jake's. Soon as Jake sees that Julia is in the building, he gradually starts winding down the practice session.

"Good job, everybody! Thursday will be harder, but I have major confidence in this group. See you all tomorrow."

The group disperses as Jake walks toward Julia. Pouring with sweat, Jake wipes off his face and head with his towel and asks Julia.

"To what be the honor of having your presence?"

Julia laughs. "Those were some great moves up here and down there."

"Down there? Ms. Julia, you have to explain where down there is?"

"Well, Mr. McKhal, I'm talking about outside. You know earlier, the whole show that was put on for free for the public's entertainment."

"Oh that, down there? It was nothing." Jake smirks and shrugs his shoulders.

"Oh really, it was nothing, huh? Well, was that nothing for anyone, Jake?"

"I don't know what you're talking about." Julia laughs and says,

"Okay then, I guess I can play hardball too." Julia begins to walk away.

"Wait, wait. Where you going, Julia?"

"Away from you, I guess."

Jake starts to laugh as he begins to open up to Julia about his performance downstairs.

"Okay, Julia, do you really want to know who the dance was for?"

"Well I didn't walk all this way across the street for nothing, Mr. McKhal."

"Alrighty then, let's go grab some lunch and—" Julia interrupts his statement.

"Wait, wait, wait. Now, where did lunch come into play at?"

"You didn't think I was just going to spill the beans right here, did you? Come on, people could be listening." Julia laughs at that comment because no one else is there in the room except them two. Then Julia pauses and reconsiders the lunch offer. She then agrees to get a bite to eat with him.

As they sit in the restaurant, they share details about themselves. Their likes and dislikes. Their goals and failures. They even take their conversation as far back as first loves. Julia is somewhat feeling guilty, but at the same time she hasn't felt so connected to anyone in a long time. Julia then asks Jake what brought him into her office the first day? Jake looks into her eyes and stares at her for a minute.

"What are you staring at?"

"I'm staring into your eyes."

"Now why would you do that?"

"That's the reason why I walked into your office in the first place."

Julia quickly puts her head down to break eye contact then says to Jake, "You couldn't see my eyes from the floor of the studio building."

"I know, that's why I came to your office, to see what color they were and I'm glad I did." Right at that moment; Julia's phone rings. It is Grant calling. In a mild panic, Julia stands up and tells Jake that she has to go now.

"Okay, wait! Julia, are we gonna do this again?"

"I don't know if I should."

"Okay, well at least give me the opportunity to take you out to eat dinner and dance the night away before I go." Jake hands Julia his business card.

"Go? Where are you going? Julia says as she takes the card

"Me and the dancers are going overseas to perform. I leave in two weeks."

Right then, a text comes through on Julia's phone. She reads the text and responds back to Grant. She text him that she is at the store getting dinner. Then she turns her attention back on Jake and tells him that he's a great guy, but she doesn't know about a next time. With a sad expression, Jake looks down at his food and watches her leave. Jake starts to think to himself that he still have two more weeks. It's either now or never.

As the days went by, Jake tries little subtle things to let Julia know that he is thinking about her. The gestures and notes were getting to Julia, but she tries to stay strong. The Sunday before Jake's final week in the States, Julia and Grant go to the movies. Before the movie starts, Grant receives a text. After reading it, he laughs and then responds back to it.

"Who was that, Grant?"

"What? The text? It is a friend of mine."

"Was it Tim?

"No Julia, it was not Tim."

"Oh." Julia says with a sarcastic voice.

"What's all that for, Julia?"

"Nothing."

"Nothing? Sounds more like sarcasm to me rather than nothing."

"Okay, then, Jake answer me this. Why do every time I ask you something you throw the first sarcastic blow?"

"First of all, I told you straight out that it is my friend, and second of all, who is Jake?"

Julia's heart jumps, but she plays it off smoothly.

"Jake? I don't know. Is that who texted you?"

"No, you just called me Jake, Julia."

"Calm down! No, I didn't Grant. You either didn't hear me or you tuned me out, like you usually do."

"Look, Julia, I don't know when date night turned into fright night, but I don't want to do this right now."

Grant then turns toward the movie screen and eats his popcorn. Julia continues to look at him with tears in her eyes. She asks him a question.

"Was it a woman who texted you?"

Grant gives a deep breath and shakes his head. "Yes, Julia. Yes, matter of fact, it was my woman's woman that texted me.

After me and you finish up here, I'm going to meet them at her house so we can start making our own movie!"

Julia slaps Grant right across the face. It takes Grant by surprise. He grabs his cheek and tosses his popcorn into Julia's lap and says, "I'm outta here!"

Grant then gets up and leaves the theater. Julia sits there angry, emotionally hurt, and crying. Julia decides it's finally time to leave. She gets up and heads toward the parking lot. Julia then sees Grant leaving out the parking structure in the car.

"Wait, Grant!" Julia shouts. "How am I supposed to get home?"

At this point she is more hurt at the fact that he leaves her, rather the fact they had a fight. Julia calls most of her friends that she know would help her out with getting home, but either they were all busy or asleep because they weren't answering their phones.

"How am I supposed to get home?" Julia says in a sullen voice.

Julia thinks long and hard about using the card that Jake had given her when they went out to eat. She really doesn't want to do it, but she concludes in her own mind that Grant left her with no choice. As she digs into her handbag, she is scrambling to find the card that she buried in there. Once she locates the card, she then nervously starts to dial Jake's number. The phone rings.

"Hello?" There is silence on the phone. Jake replies again. "Hello? Look, I'm about to hang up! Goodbye!"

"No, Jake! Wait! It's me."

"Who is me? I know a lot of people who would be me—be Julia Richards?"

"That's who me is."

"Julia? What are you doing? Calling me? I actually thought you never would."

"You were the only one left that I could think of."

"Think of for what, Julia? The time now is 10:23 p.m." Julia starts to laugh.

"Not that, you pervert! I need a ride, Jake."

"Oh, and I'm the pervert."

"Jake, it's a long story. Do you think you can come and get me?"

"Yea, that shouldn't be an issue."

"Good," Julia says as she starts to cry.

"Are you okay, Julia?"

"Long story, Jake. Long story."

"Well at least we will have something to talk about in the car."

Jake goes and picks up Julia. It was a thirty-five minute drive back to Julia's house. On the way to the house, Jake just listens. He doesn't offer advice, he doesn't interrupt, and he doesn't judge. Jake just listened. As Julia cleanes her soul, she starts to feel better about everything. When they finally arrive at Julia's home, she tells Jake that she appreciates his attentive ear. She also says, that is one quality that her husband doesn't possess. After that is said, Julia gets out of the car and tells Jake to have a good night, Jake responds with the same message.

Julia is walking up the stairs and wondering to herself, where is Grant? His car is not here. Julia shrugs her shoulders and continues to walk toward the house. As soon as she gets in, Jake drives off. Julia ready herself for bed. Before she turns off the bedroom light, she peeps out the window to see if Grant car has pulled up. When she finally stops glaring out the window, she realizes that he has not. Julia grows sad. She turns off the lights, crawls into bed and goes to sleep.

CHAPTER II

JAKE'S LAST WEEK

Grant awakens the next morning at Tim's house. After he had left the theatre the other night, he decided he was still too angry to go home, nor did he want to do anything stupid that would further ruin he and Julia's relationship.

Tim says to Grant, "Hey, buddy, now that you're here, I think now is a great opertunity for you to take my advice."

"I know, Tim, I know."

"Look man if you love your wife, you have to change or you will lose her."

"I know! I know. Just let me think, okay."

"All I'm saying is that you wouldn't have driven over here if you didn't want it to get better."

My head is starting to ache. "I need to sleep a little more."

"You do that, buddy, but don't forget that you have to be at work in four hours."

"Ouch! My head," says Grant.

Did you have to remind me?

Tim starts to laugh as he goes back upstairs to his room.

Grant suddenly awakens again, but in a state of panic. He lost track of time and just knows that he is late. The sun is shining and the birds are chirping. Usually, when he is around this type of atmosphere, he is already full steam ahead at work. Just as he expects, he should already be an hour into work. Feeling a lot better than he did a few hours ago, he quickly gathers his belongings and dashes off to work. When Grant arrives at work, Tim is outside gathering supplies from his truck.

"Hey, dork, thanks for waking me up this morning."

"Grant, I would've had an easier time waking a bear during hibernation. You wouldn't get up, Grant." Tim says as he was laughing.

"Since I come to work for money, I couldn't spend any more time on you. Besides, I covered for you. I told Harry that you had come down with something, so you're free for the day anyway. Just call and confirm what I said. Oh, and don't get seen right now, it would make me seem like a liar, and not a pretty good one at that."

Grant laughs as he continues to talk to Tim. "Thanks, man, guess I'll go clean my house and wait for Julia. Hopefully have some make-up sex."

"I don't know, buddy. You in the hole pretty deep this time."

"You're right, Tim. You know, I think I know what to do to get her to put me in the right hole." Grant starts to jog to his car as Tim is laughing.

Tim yells, "It better not be anything stupid!" Grant then heads off to Best Buy to get this camera that Julia has been wanting for three months.

Julia arrives to work at her normal time feeling almost like she has done every day for the past couple of weeks..

Dr. Reeves is already in the office. she places an elegant vase with a single red rose on Julia's desk. Dr. Reeves looks surprised to see Julia here on this particular day.

"Hey, Julia! What are you doing here?"

"Hopefully, getting ready to clock in. You not firing me, are you?" Julia asks with concern.

"No, don't be silly. You requested this day off, remember?"

It hits Julia that she did request this day off. "Oh, you're absolutely right, Monica. It must have slipped my mind."

"I remember when I was your age, honey. Too much partying on the weekend can do that to you, Julia."

Julia gives a little smirk. "Well, that for surely isn't what threw my mind off track. So do you need me to stay? I mean, I am here with nothing to do."

"Oh, Julia, you took this day off for something. Even if it's just you having some "me" time, Go ahead, get outta here."

"Okay, Monica. I'll think of something to do. Oh, and by the way Monica, nice rose. I see someone has a crush on you."

Monica snaps her fingers as she remembers the rose." Ah no, Julia. This rose isn't mine, dear. It was sent addressed to you."

Now Julia looks surprised as she finds out the beautiful rose is hers. "Really?" Julia walks toward her desk and picks up the rose. She smells the rose. Then she detaches the card that came with it. Right before she could open the card, Monica says to Julia, "This guy, crush of yours, must be young or unemployed. Where's the other eleven flowers?" Monica shakes her head in disappointment as she walks away.

Julia opens the card and it reads, "To my fair lady, I sent you one red rose. Now that you're holding it, there is a perfect pair of precious flowers in this office." This melts Julia's heart. She's overjoyed and can't help smiling. She yells out to Monica that she is finally leaving, then she exits the building. Julia then calls Jake on the phone. When he answers, she immediately tells Jake, "Teach me how to dance."

"What? When do you wanna learn? I'm leaving Saturday night.

"Is right now a good time for you, Jake?"

"You're at work, I'm at work. You just—"

Julia cuts in. "I have the day off."

This response shocks Jake. "Whoa! You want me to just lie to my dancers, skip out on rehearsals, and get behind on one day of practice to hang out with you for the day?"

"Yes, Jake. That's what I'm suggesting. I'll be exiting the building in five minutes." They both hang up. Jake makes up an excuse to cancel practice for the day and he leaves the building.

Jake and Julia are having a good time from morning until the evening. They got to know each other quite well. Julia refuses to describe or give her husband's name to Jake though. She just thinks that isn't in the best interest to do so. Jake stubbornly agrees. They end the day at a salsa club were they danced and drank. Neither of them consumes a lot of alcohol, but their body chemistry is heating up. As they dance, their bodies become entangled with one another. Their eye contact becomes fixed on each other and the signs are all there for Jake to make his move. He aggressively went in for the kiss, caressing her lower back on the dance floor, pulling her closer to him, making her realize that this date is not just going to end with a kiss, but this will be carried out until passionate love is made.

Julia wakes up to a screeching sound as a car takes off too fast from a red light outside. She glances to her left and sees Jake is still sleeping. Then she frantically checks her cell phone for the time. She quickly starts to dress and it alarms her that it's two forty-three in the morning. Jake wakes up and tells her to come back to bed. Julia is still incoherent on what took place, but she can't deny the facts that are right in front of her face. An uneasy feeling dwells in Julia's conscience about Grant finding out. She is also feeling discomfort trying to come up with a plan to get her out of this jam. She grabs her cell phone and purse then leaves the hotel room, shaken up over tonight's events.

When Julia makes it home, it is a little past 3:00 a.m. The house is quiet. There is no dripping water no television light, or no sound coming from the stereo. For some reason, the whole scene inside of her home looks eerie. She feels as though Grant knows something. As Julia lightly walks around the house, she is getting undressed. In fear that a shower would alert or awaken Grant, she chooses to sleep on the couch downstairs. She starts to settle her restless consciousness in believing that nothing is figured out. She figures tomorrow a few questions will be asked. Her plan is to have solid answers and to continue to act angry at the fact that he also stayed out all night. Julia finally falls asleep.

The alarm clock goes off sharply at seven-thirty, and Julia is definitely not feeling like rising to her feet at this time. Half in and out of drowsiness, Julia recalls the day before—the dinner with Jake, the dance with Jake, and then the night with Jake. Suddenly, she finds herself with a big satisfying smile on her face. Julia gains energy to start her day by thinking of Jake. She takes a shower, styles her hair and makeup, then she prepares some coffee. Now, Julia is off to work. Figuring that Grant has already left, she wasn't concerned when she went inside their bedroom and found it to be empty.

For the first part of the day, all Julia could think about is Jake. She doesn't want to seem obsessed, so she doesn't call or text him. She does constantly look at the studio building and wonder what is going on up there. When her break time arrives she decides to go pay Jake a visit.

Julia walks outside and right before she walks across the parking lot, Grant pulls up in front of her, blocking her path to Jake's studio building. Grant rolls down the window and starts to talk to Julia.

"Hey, baby, I missed you last night. Where were you?"

"I was with my friends, Grant."

"The whole night?"

"Yeah, and they didn't abandon me at the goddamn movies!"

"Whoa, whoa, whoa, Julia I drove all the way from work on my break to make peace with you, not to start a war."

"Okay. So where the hell did you take off to the night you ditched me?"

"Julia, I went to Tim's. I'm sorry. You know me, you know how I get. I really gotta work on my temper."

"Damn right, you do!"

"Well, you do too! Okay, I guess you don't want to talk to me right now, but I got you something." Grant reaches into the backseat and pulls out this small wrapped gift box and hands it to Julia.

"Open it," says Grant. "C'mon, open it please, Julia."

Julia opens the gift. She sees that it's the camera she wanted three months ago. She examines it and a smirk comes across her face.

"It took three months and a big fight to make you get this for me?"

Julia tosses the camera into Grant's backseat. "I'm okay. I'll just continue to use my phone for pictures."

As Julia is leaning inside the passenger side of the car talking to Grant through the window, Jake makes his way out of the studio. He is on his way to come and visit Julia. Jake is looking in the direction of Julia's parking lot and sees a woman outside of a car, talking to man inside the car. He doesn't know it is Julia. Jake then starts to cross the street. Julia stands erect, looking over the car in Jake's direction. He is heading her way. Her heart starts to pound. Julia and Jake make eye contact.

All of a sudden, the studio building doors bursts open, and one of Jake's dancers frantically yells for Jake's return. Jake hears his name being called loudly in a panicked voice. He brakes eye contact with Julia and turns to the dancer.

"What's wrong, Kim?"

"It's Amy! I think she broke her leg!"

Jake and Kim both run back into the studio to see what they can do to help Amy.

Grant is in his car when he hears Jake's name being called. Grant says the name "Jake" to himself. He is trying to figure out where he heard that name before. Julia brakes his concentration and says, "I have to go back to work."

"You didn't even eat yet?" Grant says

"I know you took my break away. It's okay though, I'll be all right."

Julia turns around and starts walking back to her work building. Grant watches her as she enters the building. He glances at the camera in his backseat and shakes his head in disappointment, then drives himself back to work.

For the next three days, Grant is growing suspicious of Julia and her whereabouts. She is glowing every day. She's being secretive and giving him incomplete answers to his questions. Grant plans a special dinner with her this Friday, and she says that she's excited to go. When Friday evening comes, Grant and Julia are both getting ready to go out. Grant says, "This is going to be great."

"What? What's going to be great?"

Grant starts to laugh at Julia's comment. Julia does not have a smile on her face. Grant then stops laughing and says, "Are you serious, Julia? We are going out right?"

"Yeah, next Friday. I didn't forget."

"Apparently, you did! I don't even know why the hell I got dressed for! Have fun, Mrs. Richards! Tell the girls, I said hello!"

Grant walks out the front door and slams it shut. He walks over to his car, gets in, and starts it up. Grant takes off and heads to the liquor store. On his way back from the store, he views his house from a distance. Grant sees Julia backing out of the driveway and he decides to follow her. Julia finally stops and parks after twenty-five minutes of driving.

Grant then comes to a complete stop, a block and a half away from Julia. He turns off his car and watches to see what she is up to. He's doing his best to follow her with his eyes, but somehow he keeps losing track of her throughout the crowd of people. He then gets out of his car and starts to walk toward the place where he seen her. All of a sudden, Julia opens the door to the bar and steps back outside. Grant quickly turns around and heads back into the direction of his car. With unclear vision working against Grant, he remembers the camera that he bought for Julia! He turns around and reaches for it out of the backseat. He uses the zoom button to see what she is doing. When Grant finally has the camera in focus, he sees she is holding a conversation with a guy. The guy is sitting on a car while conversing back and forth with Julia. Then the guy grabs Julia's arms and pulls her in for a hug. Grant takes the camera off of his face and stares from a distance in disbelief.

He then refocuses the camera to continue to view the scene. While his heart is breaking, he is glued to Julia and this mystery man, watching every little kiss and every little embrace.

Julia pulls back from Jake a little and continues her conversation with him.

"I really wish you didn't have to go, Jake. I wish you could stay here and perform. I would go to all your shows." Jake laughs a little and says, "All my shows?"

"Every last one, Jake."

Julia goes in for a kiss. Grant is trying to hold his composure in the car. Every move that Jake does to Julia has made Grant ready to fight. He somehow holds it together and continues to watch.

Julia then says to Jake, "So how long are you expected to be gone? I can handle one month but …," Jake lets her arms go and looks down at the concrete.

"Jake? How long are you going to be gone?"

After Jake takes a deep breath, he whispers to Julia, "Two, maybe three years."

Julia giggles and then says to Jake, "No really? How long are we talking? Two months … three months?"

Jake looks up from facing the concrete. He looks Julia in her eyes and says to her, "Two or possibly three years."

Julia's giggle now turns into confusion, followed by anger. She shoves Jake making him fall on the hood of the car. Jake then stands up and says,

"What the hell was that about?"

Grant is just about to get out of his car, but he decides to wait a bit longer to see how this plays out. Julia gets closer to Jake. In anger, she puts her fingers in his face.

"Why did you even talk to me if you knew you were leaving for that long?"

Then Julia steps back and says, "Oh I get it, it was never a like or dislike thing with you. You just wanted to sleep with me!"

Jake shrugs his shoulders and tilts his head to the side and says, "I thought you knew what we were."

"BAAM!" Julia slaps Jake and starts to walk away.

She turns back and yells to him, "You're wrong, Jake! You're wrong!"

"C'mon Julia! It doesn't have to end this way! What were you expecting out of this! You're married!"

Julia continues to walk away from Jake towards her car. That was the last conversation they had. Jake rubs his cheek for a minute, then he unlocks his car door and grabs some papers out. His cell phone begins to ring. In excitement he exclaims to himself. "It's Samantha!" Jake answers the phone.

"Hey, Samantha! How are you?"

Samantha jumps in rudely. "So, how is Amy?"

"Whoa, there's no. Hello Jake, how are you?"

"Look, I'm busy Jake, just got your message."

"I left that message like three days ago."

"I have a life too you now—I can leave the state or the country if I choose to." I don't belong to you.

"Look, Sam, I'm not going to fight with you tonight. I just want you to know about Amy." Samantha chimes in again.

"Yet and still you haven't told me how she is doing."

"She's fine, Sam, just fine. The only bad news is that she will not be able to come on tour with us overseas."

"Sorry to hear that, Jake. You know since this is a last-min-ute injury, it would be impossible to find a replacement, not just anyone, but someone who knows the routine. I'm sure you will think of something or someone. You always do, Jake."

"Funny you should say that, Sam, because I have thought of someone." The conversation grows quiet.

"Okay Sam, let's not play this game. I thought of you."

Sam begins to speak but Jake cuts her off.

"Let me finish please! We have no backup dancer. That means her whole routine would have to be changed! Amy is half of the show! Please if not for me, for your old team. Come to Jerry's for a drink, the gangs all here and they need you.

Come cover a couple of shows and get paid well. Then we will train someone else, then you can leave."

Samantha is quiet on the other end of the phone for a while. Then she says to Jake, "Okay, I'll have one drink. I'll hear what you have to say then I will decide."

"Thank you! Thank you! I owe you big time!"

"I'm just coming for a drink. I never said yes to the whole travel thing, okay. One thing at a time." Jake continues to talk to Samantha as he heads back into the bar.

At this time, Grant gets out of his car with the camera in hand and starts to walk toward Jake's car. As he gets closer, he starts to take pictures of the rear of Jake's car. Then he steps up to the side of Jake's car, and snaps a picture of that too. All of a sudden, he becomes full of rage and faces the bar door. Grant starts to head in the direction of the bar. He reaches for the door handle and suddenly breaks out into quiet tears. He reverses his direction and heads back to his car an emotional wreck. When Grant is secure in his car, he places the camera in the passenger seat and heads home.

Once arriving at his home, he realizes that Julia is still not home. Grant grabs the liquor he bought earlier and the camera, then he heads for the office in the house. Grant waste no time starting his drinking binge. For him not to be a drinker, starting off with this brand of alcohol is very hard for him. Bottle after bottle, he continues to drink. Recalling the events of the evening makes him want to do bodily harm to whoever this guy is. Grant connects the camera to the computer and views the photos. In his anger, he pounds the keyboard and throws objects that are on the desk across the room. In the computer desk, he finds a flash drive. He uploads the pictures to the flash and continues to destroy everything around him.

Out of nowhere, Julia steps into the office. The look on her face when she sees how much disarray the office is in, is devastating. For a split second, she is terrified. She snapped out of it and lashes out at Grant. She is not aware that he has been drinking.

"What the hell is going on, Grant!"

Grant turns to Julia with the look of amazement on his face. He gives her a look that symbolizes the phrase, "I know you didn't just ask me that!" Grant snatches the camera out of the USB port then tosses it to Julia.

"No! No! No! You have no right to ask me what the hell is wrong! You tell me, Julia! You tell me, what the hell is going on!"

Julia catches the camera and looks at it. Then she focuses on Grant and sees that his balance is off and that his speech is slurred.

She asks Grant, "Have you been drinking?" Grant looks around the disorganized office and then he looks at his alcohol bottles.

"What the hell do you think?"

"Grant, baby, calm down. You don't even know …"

Grant jumps into the conversation with fierce anger in his voice.

"Then what is all this! Augafina! You're a low-down dirty slut! How could you do this to me! I thought I would be the one to fold, I would be the one to break! But, oh no! You win, you win!"

"Grant, what are you talking about?"

"Don't play this game with me, Julia! Do not do it! I have seen you. I have seen you, guys."

Grant looks at the camera in Julia's hands and he says, "Hell, I even took some pictures!" Grant then picks up one of his bottles of alcohol and downs it. He then throws down the bottle and shatters it onto the floor. Grant starts to walk past Julia. She reaches out for his arm and catches hold of his shirt.

"I'm sorry!"

Grant snatches his arm away from Julia.

"Don't you touch me!" He is now in her face. "Do not touch me!" Grant continues to walk past Julia. She is trying to explain her actions to Grant. She finally stops talking and falls to her knees and cries while she goes through some of the pictures.

Julia then takes the camera and begins to smash it into the office room floor. She pounds on it until it breaks. She lays there on the floor in tears. She has no idea if Grant has left or if he is in the house. She doesn't want to search for him because she has never seen him this angry before.

CHAPTER III

THE PAST YEARS

Grant receives a message on his phone from Tim. The message that Tim leaves questions the well-being of Grant himself. It's been a while since Tim heard from Grant. It seems as though ever since the divorce became final, Grant just stops returning calls and hanging around his friends. Tim calls both his cell phone and his house phone, and he leaves more messages on both. When the home phone voice-machine picks up, Grant is in the den listening to what Tim has to say. Tim expresses his concern and also tells Grant that he is be stopping by to see how he is doing.

Grant just gazes at the answering machine with a blank look on his face. He sits emotionless in his favorite chair in the den. He knocks over items, papers, and a half drunken coffee cup to get to his favorite liquor bottle. After gripping the bottle firmly, he takes a sip and looks at the final divorce papers in his hands. He starts to reflect back on when things in his marriage just took a turn for the worst. Grant reminisces about the day, two years ago, when he found out about Jake.

(Flashback)

"Hey, Tim, glad you answered your cell this time."

"Yea, Carol and I were just about to eat dinner."

"You lucky pal."

"When lasagna calls my name …," Tim says

Grant jumps in, he tries to hold back the tears. "Julia is cheating on me!" The conversation grew to a close. Complete silence whispers through the phone lines for a minute. In order to break the silence, Tim asks Grant is he sure.

"I mean how do you know for certain, Grant?"

"I have pictures. I've seen it with my own two eyes, and most importantly she didn't bother to try and deny it when I confronted her."

"I'm sorry, Grant. Sorry you're going through this. Look, I can meet you at the—," Grant jumps in.

"Naah," his voice shaky. "You don't have to meet me any-where. I don't wanna ruin the good thing you and Carol got going." Grant laughs sarcastically thinking about his situation.

"It will be no problem, Grant. What do you think friends are for?"

"Meet me at Jerry's—,"

"Nooooo! I won't go to Jerry's! I will not drink there!"

"Okay, okay. Calm down, man. We don't have to go there."

"Look, Tim, I just need someone to talk to for a brief min-ute. Besides, I'm drunk enough for the both of us already."

"Here we go," says Grant. "The Daisy Inn. Tim, I just need to sleep. I wanna go to sleep. You treat Carol right, and damn it have some babies already! You know she wants babies, and if you don't help her, this jerk sleeping with my wife will! Goodnight, Tim." Grant hangs up.

Tim holds the phone to his ear for a minute, and then he tells Carol briefly what is happening. Also during Carol and Tim's conversation, Tim is getting ready to go find Grant. Tim kisses Carol, tells her that he loves her so much and when he gets home, they are going to start making babies.

Tim knows exactly where The Daisy Inn is at. He use to go there a lot in his high school days. Once Tim arrives at the inn, he spots Grant's car and pulls up beside it. Tim gets out of the vehicle and hears a thumping noise coming from room 110. It sounds like Grant yelling at the TV screen over a football game. When Grant hears a knock on his door, he quiets himself to see where the knocking is coming from.

(Flashback ends.)

Grant snaps out of it and realizes that right now someone is knocking on his home door with a stern voice. Grant yells "Who's there?"

"It's me, Tim."

Grant looks around the room and sees the condition in which things are. The house is a mess. He yells out to Tim, "Why didn't you call first? I could have cleaned some stuff up for you. Now I have nowhere for you to sit," Grant says in a buzzed voice.

"I don't mind sitting in filth, I'm a guy, remember?"

"Okay, you have been warned." When Grant opens the door, Tim gives him a hug. Tim is excited that he gets this opportunity to talk to Grant. Knowing how stubborn Grant is, he wants to get in as much quality time as possible.

"Wow, Grant! Look at this place."

"You're not supposed to kick a man when he is down, but not only did you kick that man, you also broke his legs so he could not get back up."

"Well, we got a long day ahead of us."

"What do you mean, Tim?"

"This place isn't gonna clean itself up now, is it? We can clean and talk. Just like old times."

"We never cleaned and talked before, Tim."

"Old times have to originate from somewhere. I guess this is where ours will start." Grant laughs and starts to pick up items around the house.

About the twenty-minute mark, Grant decides to share some information with Tim.

"I remember about a month or so after the whole Jake thing was discovered, Julia and I started to go to counseling. It seemed as though the counselor gave me the most hell. Probably, because I'm a guy. We came home from our session, and Julia wanted me to put into practice what the counselor just told us to do. Me, being who I am, I didn't easily give in to her demands."

(Flashback.)

"So Grant, I hope I didn't make you feel pressured, but it's been about an hour now and you never told me how the food taste."

"Are you serious, Julia? Food?"

"Hey, that's not fair. The counselor said to start small. She said brownie points can add up to big rewards."

"I don't know if I can wait that long, I want my reward now! Who is this jerk you were messing with? What's so hard about giving me a name?"

"C'mon, Grant, we know pretty much the same people. I know what you can get out of a name and who can give you that 'names' information! Was my food good, I know you hear me! Answer my question!"

"Fine! I'm leaving!" Right as Julia starts to walk out the door, Grant yells.

"You wanna know the truth? The food was so-so!" Julia turns around and looks at Grant like he just gave the wrong answer.

"So-so? So-so? Did you know I got that recipe from your mother yesterday?" Julia picks up her keys and throws them at Grant. He dodges the keys and runs to go and pick them up.

"I am so leaving now!" says Julia.

"Not so fast, Julia, just that quickly you forgot what you threw at me?"

"Crap! Grant, give me my keys."

"Nope you gotta come and get them," says Grant.

"Look, Grant, I'm upset with you, and this behavior of yours is not making it any better."

Grant jiggles the keys and tells Julia to come and get them.

Grant starts to make her laugh by tickling her. She tries to keep her anger streak going, but she breaks out into a smile and laughter and tackles Grant onto the floor. They lock eyes and they begin to kiss. Grant then offers the keys to Julia. She takes the keys out of his hands and tosses them near the front door. They continue to kiss as they playfully wrestle.

(Flashback ends.)

"At that moment, after that evening, I thought we were going to last. I thought we were going to survive this thing." Grant holds back a couple of tears as he continues to talk to Tim.

Hours had gone by, Tim and Grant cleans and straightens up all that is disorganized. The den is the only room left to be cleansed. They continue to talk. Tim is trying to cheer Grant up by staying only on the memories of good rather than bad.

"We had some good times together, huh, Grant? I guess sometimes things change for a reason. For instance, take you for an example. In these past two and a half years, I've seen some remarkable changes in you. Your listening became attentive, your temper decreased when arguing, and your sarcasm has lessened. And the most important thing that I see, is that the love for your wife grew. It's like multiplied tenfolds."

"But if you see these things, Tim, why doesn't she? Why doesn't she focus on what I am doing right? I love her! I never stepped out, or crossed the borders of our marriage. Yeah, I was tempted, but who hasn't been." Grant starts to cry now.

"After all I've done, she couldn't even tell me face to face that she was done trying. Why couldn't she at least have done that?" Grant knocks over what just been neatly arranged in the den. Tim raises his voice in anger at Grant.

"Calm down, man, maybe going down memory lane is not such a good thing for you after all. From now on, lets you and me just stay in reality that is today."

"I like my misery, Tim. It brought me my own personal happiness. I just loath around the house. Why did you come over, Tim? Why did you steal my happiness?"

"I'm here because my friend, since the beginning of time, needs my help. You're hurting, Grant, and since I can't feel what you feel, I'm at least trying to soften the blow."

"Well, it ain't working," says Grant.

Grant reaches for the open bottle of alcohol and starts to guzzle it down. Tim makes way over to Grant and snatches it out of his hands.

"This is why you loath! This is why you're miserable! For two years, I have watched you grow to be a better man. Now, in two months I've seen you become far worse off than you've ever been."

Grant shoves Tim onto the couch. Tim gets up and starts to have words with Grant. After Tim breaks the bottle on the floor out of anger, Grant shakes his head and laughs, then he begins a conversation with Tim.

"You're right, Tim. We have known each other for a long time. We go way back. Maybe, just maybe everything in life has to change."

"So what are you saying, Grant?"

"First off, I'm saying I love you like a brother, hell, my only brother. Secondly, get the hell out of my house!"

"What?"

"Get the hell out! I knew I wasn't ready for visitors!"

"You want me out, Grant? Fine, I'm out! I'm not sticking around here where I'm not wanted." Tim heads toward the door.

"And close the damn door when you're gone!

As Grant hears the door slam, he immediately turns all of his anger into destruction. He throws stuff around the den, he snatches pictures off the wall, and he grabs his other alcohol bottle out of the drawer. Then he flips the computer desk over. All the paper, pictures, and valuables fall out of the desk and onto the floor. Grant walks to the corner of the room, he sits there and he drinks. He starts to reminisce on the day he got the letter.

BEFRIENDED

(Flashback)

The following day of the heated argument, Grant went to work as usual. All throughout the day, he worries about Julia. She claims to have left the heated conversation to go get some milk, but never returns home that night. Grant figures by the time he gets home if she still isn't there, he will call the police. Upon arriving at his doorstep, he brings in the mail from today. It concerns Grant that neither Julia nor her car was at the house. Right when he was about to dial 911, he looks at one of the letters in the mail. The letter doesn't have a stamp on it and it was in Julia's handwriting. He quickly reaches for it and began reading. It said:

Dear Grant,

I don't know how to start this letter, but I guess it has to begin somewhere. It seems as though more tears than ink are getting on this paper because I now know what must happen to US. In order to survive this life, I know that we must do it apart. We have been together for a long time. Maybe our time together is not supposed to be forever. Maybe we were both put together to get us both through rough parts in our lives. By the time you read this, I would have been on my way somewhere for about a day now. I'm sorry for the hurt that I have caused you, and I know that you really tried to make it work. Who knows, maybe somewhere down the road, we will meet again, and this time, maybe we will be forever.

Goodbye, Grant.
Take care of yourself.

(Flashback over)

Grant staggers backwards until he leans onto the wall for support. He finally manages to stand upright in the corner. Grant picks up an open liquor bottle and begins to drink.

"How the hell am I supposed to take care of myself! That's like shooting me in the foot and telling me to walk to the store for some Band-Aids!"

Now, feeling a little buzz, Grant goes for another swig of his drink. The bottle slips out of his hand, lands on his foot, and rolls into the pile of paperwork and junk that was knocked out of the overturned drawer.

Grant falls to the floor in an uncomfortable pain due to the bottle hitting his foot. Then he rubs his foot for a while. When his foot feels a little better, he then positions himself on his knees and starts to crawl where his bottle has rolled to. He picks up the bottle and drinks some more. As he was about to stand, he notices a photo of him and Julia at the Grand Canyon. He picks up the photo and recounts the events for that day. Then he cocks his head to the left and squints his eyes, and notices something that he hasn't seen in years. Grant grabs the flash drive that was under the picture and he prays that it is the same one he used two years prior. He crawls over to the computer and fixes it up in functional condition. Then he turns it on and inputs the flash drive. He opens some files and none seem to be what he is looking for. Grant runs across an unnamed file and clicks on it.

A big smile comes across his face as he sees the pictures of Julia and Jake at the bar two years ago. Then he goes to the other picture and pulls up the one with Jake's license plate on it. Grant is excited and angry at the same time. He knows people who can help him unlock the mystery of Jake. Now, armed with a little information about the man who helped destroy his life, all that is on Grant's mind is to bring harm to him in any way possible.

CHAPTER IV

GRANT MEETS JAKE

After four days, Grant returns back to his associate to pick up the information on Jake. After Grant pays the man what he was owed, the man gives Grant the files that could locate Jake McKhal. When Grant got into his car, he wasted no time digging into his files, skimming through sentences, and peeking through pictures. He just wants an address. He just wants to be face to face with Jake. Grant finally came across an old work address and it sounds familiar. Grant starts his car and proceeds to track him down. Grant instantly remembers where he's going. He becomes enraged in the car because that building is close to Julia's old job. Once he arrives at the address, he steps out of the car and glances at Julia's old workplace. He's then hit with a flashback of, when Julia and him were talking in the parking lot and he heard someone yell out "Jake, Jake." He shakes his head and can't imagine why he didn't put it all together then.

Grant then continues to head toward the Empire Towers where Jake's studio was located. As he reaches the front desk of the Empire Tower, the security guard welcomes Grant and asks him how he can direct him to where he has business at. Grant then proceeds to engage in conversation with the security guard. He asks the female security guard where in this building is Dance Studio 3.

"Dance Studio 3?" The guard said with a confused expression on her face. "Uhm, I'll have to look in the directory and see if that is even located here, sir." As she was checking the building directory for Dance Studio 3, her replacement guard came in a little early to prepare for the shift change.

"Hello, Becky!" no yelling

"Hello Lynn! I didn't expect to see you today. I thought you were off today, Lynn."

"I know yesterday I told you that I was, but I need the money. So here I am. So what are you looking up, Becky?"

"The gentleman in front of me would like to know if there is a Dance Studio 3 in this building." Lynn starts to think for a second, and then she remembers and blurts out, "Jake!" Grant's eyes opened wide as he become filled with joy. He's on to Jake's whereabouts. Now, it's all a matter of time." Then Lynn said, "Oops! Did I say that out loud?" She giggles.

"Nah, it's okay. So you do know where Dance Studio 3 is located?

"Well, yeah it was here like two years ago. Then they left for a tour."

"They took off on tour?"

"I guess they got booked on some international gigs or something. Jake told me 'bye on their last day here, then they left."

"So you knew Jake?"

Lynn smiles as she thinks about times that she spent with Jake, she snaps out of it and says to Grant.

"I knew him a little."

"Do you know where I can find him?"

"I'm his friend," says Grant. "A long lost friend."

"Then how come you don't know where he is?"

"I told you, I'm long and lost."

"I'm sorry, sir, but I can't disclose any more information about Jake to you."

Right as Lynn said that, Anna who was just finishing her rounds walked by the front desk. Not knowing of the conversation that just took place between, Grant, Becky, and Lynn.

Anna walks up to the desk with excitement and says to Becky, "Guess what, girl, speaking of Jake, he just facebooked me! He's back from China now!" Anna was the one that took Jake's attention from Lynn, and she despised Anna for it.

"So what, Anna, he facebooked me too!"

"Liar! He just got back today. He told me that he just reopened his account because his wife is the jealous type!

As the conversation was going on, Grant pulls out his phone at the counter. He scoots a little to the left and pretends he is on a phone call. He listens attentively so he can get more clues on where Jake is. After two minutes of the girls bickering back and forth, Grant goes for the kill. "Hey, so did Jake tell you where Dance Studio 3 has moved to now? I guess he didn't tell Lynn." Without missing a beat, Anna says, "Yeah, it's on 3rd and Pixel." Grant smiles and says, "Thank you, Anna." Grant left the two girls bickering as he is now headed to 3rd and Pixel.

A lot of things were going through Grant's mind. The last thing to go through his mind was joy. That only entered his thoughts because, he was now about to physically meet the guy who started the downward spiral to his marriage. The closer he gets to 3rd and Pixel, the more enraged he became. Grant has no initial plan. He just knows that he wants to hurt Jake bad. Now killing him was not in the plan, but with Grant's emotions really heating up, he didn't know what might end up of this day.

Grant finally reaches 3rd and Pixel, and he hops out of his car. He walks calmly to the front doors of the building. Grant is now scooping the scene around him and the building itself. There seems to be no one around at this time. The closer Grant gets to the building, he notices how it's not quite finished yet in construction. When Grant reaches the double-glass doors, he pulls on them. This unsettles Grant because they are locked. Once again he thinks that somehow Jake alludes him.

Grant then peeks into the building and scans the inside for clues of the studio. He sees unfinished walls, electrical material, plumbing material, and some data material. On the back right hand corner of the unfinished building, he sees the proof that he needs to know that this is where Jake will dwell. A big neon sign of Dance Studio 3 is sitting on the floor waiting to be installed outside. Grant steps back and smiles that this is it. Jake will be here. It's all a matter of time. The security guard pulls up to Grant on his golf cart and asks Grant to clear the area. Grant quickly thinks of a plan. He tells the security guard that he works for Intel Communications. He was just checking to see if the materials were delivered. The guard then drives away as he took Grant's word for it. At that very instant, Grant gets an idea. That's how he would get in. He would use the cover of his job and the unfinished building to get him close to Jake. Grant finally returns back to his car and heads for home. He figures it's the best place to come up with an idea.

Grant goes home, drinks, looks at his old wedding album, and conceives a vicious plan. The only thing he was able to come up with in the four hours of his planning was to stab him. That way, he has a better chance of survival but he will be left with a scar to remind him of other people's pain. So in Grant's drunken state of being, he practices stabbing someone. He practiced on the air, he practiced on a pillow, and then he upgrades to a teddy bear that he won at the fair. He puts Jake's picture on that bear and went at it. He finally realises where he wants to strike, so he concentrates on the lower abdominal area.

Grant awakes the following day at around 10:00 a.m. He jumps out of bed a little buzzed, but ready to sease this momment. He figures he is going to get caught. He figures he will do time, but the time won't hurt as bad as the time that he is doing right now emotionally. Grant got ready as though he was preparing for work. He takes the sharpest, concealable pocket knife that he has and heads toward the door. The only thing Grant was thinking about was that he totally has nothing else to lose.

Grant pulls up into the parking lot of Dance Studio 3. He looks in the studios direction and sees construction work being done. He hopes that Jake would have come to see the progress of the building. Grant has no idea how this would play out. He knows that he just wants this over with. Grant begins to walk toward the building with his work badge showing and his weapon in his pocket. He approaches the doors, and proceeds to walk in. There was loud noise to be expected and obstacles to overcome before finding Jake. Grant goes up to the electrician and asks, "Is Jake here?"

The electrician said, "Jake Nelson or Jake McKhal?" Grant has to think quickly. "You know the one with no dance moves who owns this establishment." The electrician laughs and says, "Okay, you talking about McKhal then." The electrician looks past Grant as he is skimming the premises, then he spots Jake. He tells Grant to turn around and make a right at the corner hall. He just seen him go that way.

Grant turns and faces the direction in which Jake has gone. As he approaches the hallway, he can hear a man on the cell phone arguing with a contractor. Grant's heart starts to pound heavily. He places one hand in his pocket and grips the knife. The closer he gets to the corner, the louder the man on the phone seems to become. Grant is thinking of the pain, he's thinking of the compromising positions Julia might have been in with his jerk. Grant is thinking about the time and effort he put into his marriage, and all because of this guy, his wife is no more.

When Grant turns the corner, all he can hear are his own footsteps. All he can see is Jake on the phone. Everything else tunes out, even the work that is being done in the room behind Jake isn't even visible to Grant. All Grant can see or concentrate on is this moment.

Jake looks Grant square in the eyes and then turns away. Still engaged in his conversation, he doesn't know what Grant's motives are. He thinks Grant is another worker doing his job.

Now, with Grant's hands submerged in sweat and with hatred in his heart, he is now inches from Jake. With Jake's back fully exposed to Grant, he began to launch into his attack.

Just before Grant can get the knife out of his pocket, the electrical box on the wall that's in the room with Jake and the other workers produces a huge spark. Wires inside the box starts to burn and a cloud of smoke fills the room. A fire is starting to flare up. Jake drops his phone in shock and stares at the box in panic.

Grant drops the knife and pushes Jake out of the way as he heads for the main breaker in that room. With all of the power going out in that suite, Grant still has enough light to find the switch and shut it off. He then grabs the fire extinguisher from the wall and put out the fire.

After Grant has done all of this, the electricians finaly makes it over to the panel. They were arguing amongst each other pointing blame at one another. Jake's concern at this time was for the guy who put out the fire. In Jake's panic, a stranger just might have saved his establishment. Jake went over to talk to the hero of the day.

"Hey!" Jake extends his hand for a handshake. "Thanks, buddy. I don't know what would've happen to my place if you weren't here."

Grant looks at his hand as if it were cursed. He didn't want to shake the man's hand who ruined his life, he wanted to break it. For a split second, Grant saw that Jake's was catching onto his facial expression and he starts to think quick. Grant then extends his hand and apologizes for the late response. He says he was in shock still from the event that just took place.

"So, are you all right now, man?" Jake asked.

"Yeah, I'm fine," says Grant.

"My name is Jake, Jake McKhal. Once again, thank you, Grant." Jake looks at Grant's name. "I'll be letting your boss know about this. Is he here?"

"Uhm, nah. Actually, I'm on a project down the road that just finished up. I came by this sandwich place last week and seen your sign through your window. I'm thinking this would be a great way to meet the ladies." They both laugh.

"Well, you're right about that Grant. I've met plenty of ladies doing what I do."

"You, lucky guy, you. I bet some hot married ones have come your way too."

"Tall, black, white, single, lesbian, married I had them all," Jake says. They laugh for a little bit and then Jake asked Grant a question.

"So you're not an electrician, how did you know what to do?"

"I wanted to be an electrician years back. I took a course and learned a lot. I ended up doing communications because it's a tad bit easier. I did what I did off sheer adrenaline, I guess. I saw trouble. I tried to end trouble. I'm glad that it worked out," Grant says.

"So tell me this, Grant? Do you know anything about sound prep work?"

"Yeah, I picked up some along the way. What's up?"

"Well, the jerk on the phone has screwed me for the last time. He is part of the reason we didn't stay international for three years. In the beginning, he was great. Somewhere down the line he lost it. I don't know, maybe it was the booze and the women. Anyway, he didn't show up again. He was supposed to prep the equipment. I can't count on him anymore, Grant. I need someone I can trust."

"Well, Jake to be honest with you, I don't know. My schedule might not work out for you, better yet for me, and we don't really know each other. I mean, I'm grateful that I was able to put your fire out, but I have to think about it."

"Okay, Grant, that's understandable. In all aspects you are right. I know I need someone soon. Take my card. If you change your mind call me. I'll be looking for someone else to fill the position, but if you call and it's still available, It's yours."

"Thanks for the opportunity, but I don't think I will be calling."

Right after Grant had said that, Jake extends his hand for a final handshake. Grant reluctantly shakes Jake's hand. Then Grant turns and walks away from the room.

Grant had made it to the front doors of the studio. He was sort of disappointed in himself for not going through with his plan. Even though he thinks to himself that he just might have save someone, he's angry Jake was unharmed in his visit. Grant then exits the building and then heads to his car. A piece of paper that is blowing in the wind wraps around Grant's leg. He looks up and realizes that there are papers flying everywhere. He spots the origin of the papers. They are coming from the trunk of a car. Grant notices a beautiful young woman bent over inside the car, searching for something in the backseat. Grant is checking out every portion of her body that he can see, from her long amatory legs, to her plush curvy backside.

Grant snaps out of the trance and began to signal for the lady's attention.

"Excuse me, ma'am." Samantha hears someone that sounds like they are trying to get her attention. She removes herself from the car, just as Grant expected. She was gorgeous as her physique has made her out to be. Standing at 5'6", green eyes, long dark hair and a smile that would paralyze anyone that stares for too long. She was a woman worth keeping as far as the "vision test" goes.

Samantha response to Grant. She asks him, "Were you trying to get my attention?"

"Yes, ma'am, I was. Your papers are flying out of your trunk."

Samantha looks into her trunk and sees her financial records blowing all over the place. Grant picks up the paper that was on his leg, and then he helps gather the rest.

As Grant is handing her a few of the papers he's retrieved, Jake comes running out of the building. He starts chasing down the paper that he sees, making its way across the street. Once Jake grabs the paper, he turns to Samantha and says, "You see why I tell you not to leave these papers in the trunk! Sometimes you be killing me, Samantha."

"I'm sorry, Jake. I had no idea that it was this windy outside." Jake finally stands face to face with Samantha. "If it wasn't for Grant helping you out, we'd be missing a ton of valuable information. Lucky I see like an owl and spotted you."

Jake turns his attention from Samantha and toward Grant. "You must be my guardian angel." Grant laughs at that comment.

"Grant, this is my wife, Samantha."

"Hi, Grant," says Samantha.

"This is the second time you've saved my business. I think we were destined to work together." Once again Grant laughs at the comment and says, "Well …," Jake jumps in. "Just think about it. If it's available it's yours."

Grant says, "I'll think about it." Grant then proceeds to his car as Samantha and Jake talk.

Grant turns back around to look at them. The way that Jake came across earlier on Samantha reminded him of when he used to come across too strong on Julia. Grant then turns back around shaking his head. As soon as Grant sat in his car, he became emotional. He began to let tears flow down his cheeks. Upset and hurt as Grant was, he snatches the picture of Julia and him off of his dashboard. His eyes start to water more heavily as he looks at the picture of the fun-filled day at the Grand Canyon. That day was so beautiful, so serene. Grant began to rip the picture down the middle. He balls it up in two pieces and throws the two halves to the floor of the car. He then lie there on the steering wheel with his eyes closed, and only his thoughts. When he opens his eyes, he sees the half-torn picture. He is looking at his half of the picture. Suddenly he lifts his head from the steering wheel. He grabs the half-torn picture of himself and looks at it. From the top of his eyes, he looks at Dance Studio 3 building. He quickly peeks right. He spots Jake and Samantha. As they laugh and talk, Jake gives her a hug and kiss. Then he tries to cuddle with his wife. She playfully pushes him away. Jake and Samantha stand about three feet apart of each other and continue to converse. All the while Grant has a new plan, it's not a plan of murder; it's not even a plan of physical pain. Grant takes the torn picture of him and holds it up, blocking Jake out of sight. The only picture Grant sees now is of Samantha and him. Grant takes the picture down. He smiles, turns on his car, and heads for home. Grant says to himself, An eye for an eye, a wife for a wife.

CHAPTER V

TIME TO GO TO WORK

A whole week passes, and Grant knows exactly what he has to do to retaliate against Jake. He knows that his open invitation to work for him was running out of time, so he plans to act quickly. Saturday that was approaching seem to be an opportune time for Grant to call Jake. He figures that Jake would be off and more easily to get in contact with. Grant calls Jake, and was right on the money. Jake answered his phone.

"Hello?"

"Hello Jake, it's me, Grant."

"Hey, buddy! You decided to call after all! So what's up? Shoot me the skinny."

"Well, I've been thinking about your offer, Jake. It seems pretty tempting and I can always use the side money."

"It's great to hear from you, Grant! So you saying you're all in?"

"Right now I'm saying, I'm in! I still want to meet with you to discuss matters of hours, days, and pay. You know stuff like that."

"Oh, okay, no problem. Hey, can you meet at the office on Monday around 11:00 a.m.?"

"That time is no good for me, Jake. Let's make it 3:30 p.m."

"Okay, cool. I can do that."

"All right it's a deal then. I'll see you then Jake, bye." Jake and Grant hang up with each other. Now his plan is in motion.

All throughout the weekend, Grant has been anxious for Monday. He's been up all weekend going over ideas and thinking up plots and plans out to completion. He always manages to find faults in his own plans though. That's why he has so many scenarios of how things are going to pan out. Come tomorrow, Grant has to decide on one plan because tomorrow is the day.

Grant awakens around his normal time on Monday morning. He calls into work and takes the day off. He lingeres around his house until it is time for him to dress up. Once he dresses, Grant leaves his house to go meet up with Jake. Upon arrival, he notices that the exterior of the building was coming along. Grant steps inside and seen how nice the interior is looking. He asks some of the workers there which way to Jake's office. They promptly give him directions and he heads out to Jake's office.

As Grant was approaching the office door, he hears what sounds to be a conversation taking place. He kinda put his ear a little closer to the door. He now hears Samantha and Jake talking about dinner arrangements that they have set up among some friends. Right then he began to get nervous all over again, but he is determined not to let this stop him. Grant then begins to fix his shirt a little and makes sure his appearance is in order. Then he knocks on the office door and waits for Jake to tell him to come in.

"Hello, Jake. Hi, Samantha. I wasn't expecting to see you here."

"Well, I wasn't expecting on staying long. I was just in the neighborhood and I had some things I had to discuss with my hubby. Oh! And you can call me Sam."

"Baby, I thought that name was only restricted to me and intermediate family?"

"Hmm, do I detect a little jealousy, Jake?"

"He can call you whatever he wants except for His and Sam." Grant kinda laughs at the comment.

"It's okay, Samantha, I think I'll be sticking with that. I don't want to get fired before I get the job." They all laugh. Samantha stands up and tells Jake she is about to go home. She then exits the room and tells Grant that it was nice to see him again. Grant grinned and said, "Likewise."

After Samantha left, Grant then took a seat, and began to discuss this business endeavor with Jake. They talk for about forty minutes. During that time, they work out the scheduling, the hours, and the pay. Everything sounded good to both parties. Grant then stands up, and tells Jake that he think it will be a pleasure working by his side. Immediately, Jake responds back to Grant, "Say, are you hungry?"

"Well, I ate before I got here."

"C'mon, grub is on me. I'm new to this area, and that fish house down the street looks great."

"Well …" Grant hesitates for a while. Okay sure, why not." They get in Jake's fancy Mercedes and head to the fish house.

Once they arrive, they step out of the car and approach the hostess. She sits them down. Jake receives a text from Samantha. He reads the text and smirks while shaking his head. Then begins to speak to Grant.

"Jealous? I'm not jealous." Grant looks confused.

"What are you talking about, Jake?"

"Nothing. Well, Sam sent me this text saying that I was jealous earlier."

"When? Oh with the whole name thing, huh?"

"Yeah, but I don't look at that as a jealous act."

"I just look at that as an earned reward."

"I mean, no offense to you Grant, but you only met her twice and spoke to her for a total of four minutes max, am I right?"

"Right, you are Jake. I understand where you are coming from. I wouldn't want no one to call my wife my cuddle name that I have for her either."

"Good, so I'm not alone in this matter then." They both laugh.

"Plus, I know my wife. If she wasn't married to me, you would be her type."

"I would?"

"Yeah, I'm the first guy close to her age that she's ever dated."

"Wow! No kidding?"

"Tell me about it," says Jake.

"She thinks guys her age aren't on her level. We're too immature, she says."

"Then what made her marry you?"

"Look at me, are you kidding?" They both laughed.

"Me and Samantha have history."

(Flashback)

Everyone is practicing in the studio in China. They are getting ready for next week's show. Jake leaves the group of dancers who he was working with and heads over into Samantha's location. Samantha is in her own world on the dance floor, twisting and turning. She looks fabulous as she spins and moves her body. Jake is watching from a close distance. Unbeknownst to Samantha, she continues to grace the floor. Jake finally decides to let his presence be known and approaches Samantha with applause. Her concentration is broken up by this. She turns to see who is applauding her, and smiles when she notices that it is Jake.

"So did you like that one move I did?"

"Yes I did, you just added that in, huh?"

"I was thinking that the extra spin would get the crowd more into the performance. Believe me, Sam, if it got me into the performance from over there, the audience will love it." Samantha laughs and tells Jake to hush. With a smile on her face, she then asked Jake to watch a bit of her new routine she has put together. Jake agreed. He was attentively watching Samantha as she dances. Three minutes into her dance bit, Jake's phone rings. He looks at the phone and notices that it is Rebecca. Jake takes the call. Before leaving, he makes eye contact with Samantha. Samantha continues to dance for a while longer, but her focus was gone. She starts to stumble and becomes offbeat with the song. Her eyes follow Jake as he continues to move farther and farther away from her. By the looks of it, Samantha has concluded it to be a fling of Jake's and they are in a heated argument.

Jake, while still on the phone, looks up to view Samantha as she dances. All Jake sees at this point is a silhouette of Samantha leaving out of the exit doors. Jake abruptly interrupts Rebecca's rant on the phone and tells her to never call him again. Without waiting for a response, Jake hangs up the phone and runs to the exit doors to catch up with Samantha. He makes it out of the doors and into the hallway where she sits in tears. Samantha looks up and notices Jake. She then quickly stands up and begins to walk into the women's locker room. Jake loudly and boldly shouts out her name.

"Samantha!" she continues to walk into the locker room and Jake follows her. He touches her shoulder to turn her around, and she does due to the force of the touch. She turns around and shoves Jake exclaiming, "Get the hell out of here! You don't belong in the women's locker room or my life!"

"You got some nerve, Jake! I hate you!"

"You hate me? For what Sam, because I was on my phone! Why don't you just ask who I was talking to?" Samantha gathers her things out of the locker room.

"So where are you going? Are you abandoning the tour?"

"No, Jake, just you. I'm leaving behind everything about you."

Now as they enter the hallway, Jake speeds up and steps in front of Samantha. He is standing between her and the doorway.

"Can you move, please?" Samantha says with tears in her eyes in a low tone voice

"No. I don't want you to leave me."

"Jake, we both know, I mean nothing to you. I'm just another piece, just like all the rest. We've been out here for like a year and half. I couldn't even begin to count the women I've seen you with, and two days ago, you just added me back to your rap sheet. Not anymore, Jake. Not anymore." Samantha wipes her eyes free from her tears. Then Jake attempts to touch her face, she blocks his hand and tells him to move. Jake refuses to move so she shoves him out of the way and reaches for the door. Jake yells out to Samantha as she opens the door.

"I love you!" It was so loud, the practicing dancers hears his statement. Samantha continues to walk out the door and into the studio. Loudly, Jake says, "Can I have everyone's attention." Samantha continues to walk. "Now, this phone I hold in my hand is the newest, the greatest iPhone out to date. It has helped me connect with a lot of women, even some of you in here. I'm done with it." Jake heaves the phone to the floor, shattering it into pieces. Samantha stops and turns around to see what that was. Jake continues to talk, "I can get a new phone that is no problem. I did that to get rid of all contacts that would keep me and Samantha apart. Sam, you haven't heard from me for a whole day because I've been cutting ties with people. Earlier, when I was on the phone, that was one of my last. Now, by breaking my iPhone, I sped up the process. I just want you."

"No you don't, Jake! You think that's what you want! You visualize us together for a brief moment, and then you're gone. Probably not gone physically, but your heart always checks out first."

Jake stands by quietly and starts to look at his group, they are all tuned in. They want to see what Jake's next move is. Jake then takes his attention off the group, and begins to look Samantha right in her eyes. Then he begins to speak.

"Samantha, I know talk is cheap. All I do is talk. That's what I'm good at. I'm changing. Well, at least I believe I am. I'm changing to be a better man for you. Don't freak out! This is not going to turn into any proposal. I know we are far from that. All I want you to do is give me a shot. You know what they say, 'Children do what children do, but a man does what a child cannot.' I'm all grown up, Samantha. Let's make us happen."

Samantha wipes more tears from her eyes as the crowd remains mute. She stares at some of the women dancers that she knows has had encounters with Jake. Two of the dancers tear up and leave, but the rest of the crowd begins to come alive with optimistic feedback. Samantha propels herself into Jake's directions and stops inches from his face. There he stood 6'2", looking down into the eyes of his 5'6" counterpart. She looks up at him with fear in her eyes, but with courage to face it in her heart. She then lounges into an emotional hug with Jake and burst into tears aloud. The dancers start to clap, and Jake tightly embraces Samantha.

(Flashback ends.)

Jake begins to speak to Grant.

"After that moment, I've been giving it my all to be a one-woman man, and it's been working. A couple of months after that, I proposed and of course she said yes. And that's where we are today, eight months married."

"Wow! That is a beautiful story, man." The waiter brings their food to the table and they continue to talk as they eat. Grant then picks up a spoonful of soup as he asks Jake another question. "So after all that, Jake, do you regret being with any of the women you were with?"

"Nope. Not a one. Every single 'fling' helped me to become who I am."

"Well, what about the married women at least? Do you feel bad for probably helping to ruin their marriages?" Grant asks Jake while looking down at his food and eating.

"Not any one of them either. Some husbands weren't performing their marital duties efficiently, so that's where I filled

As the weeks go by, Grant becomes a little more relaxed in his role as sound coordinator. Jake is taking a liking to him as an employee and as a friend. Grant has sat down with Jake and Samantha on some occasions to have lunch with them, and Grant continues to play it smooth. Not showing any interest in Samantha beyond a work relationship, he was waiting for the right moment to set off his plan.

On Friday of Dance Studio 3 grand opening, everyone was excited. No longer would they have to rent out studios. No longer would they have to commute to various locations. They were overjoyed that the project was complete.

The first day of rehearsal went really well. Jake leaves everyone dehydrated and exhausted. He feels as though the moves were not solid yet. Not everyone was in sync with one another. Jake wants to fix that. As the dancers dance their hearts out, Grant works the sound equipment almost flawlessly. As the rehearsal was taking place, Samantha walks in. Unaware of her presence, Grant was feeling the vibe of the music. Even thought he has no rhythm nor dance moves, he tries the best he could to dance with what skills he has.

Grant then hears laughter come from behind him. He quickly stops dancing and turns around. Grant begins to laugh at the fact that he got caught dancing or lack thereof. Samantha begins to speak to Grant.

"So you call that dancing, huh? She giggles as she speaks.

"Hey, they may not be the prettiest moves, but they are mine. I own these." They both start laughing. Samantha looks him in the eyes and says, "Maybe one of these days I'll show you how to move." Grant is speechless. He has no reply or comment.

Jake finally notices Samantha talking to Grant, and he breaks routine with the dancers and shouts out. "So Sam, what happened in the meeting?" Grant hears Jake utter words over in his direction, so he shuts the music off. The dancers fall to the floor in exhaustion. Some run for water, while others head outside for fresh air. Jake repeats himself. "So what happened, Sam?"

in for them." Grant drops his spoon into his soup by accident, he wasn't expecting that answer from Jake.

"So you just happen to be the right man for the job, huh. The rent-a-husband," Grant says with a stern voice.

"Yea, I guess you can say that. I got no complaints."

Grant begins to look up from his food and stares at Jake. Eye to eye. The waiter then comes and places their main meal on the table. Jake breaks eye contact and begins to look at his own food.

"Man, I'm starving! Okay, Grant, enough about my past. Let's work on our future endeavors."

"Yeah, let's do that, Jake. Let's switch gears." Jake then goes and tells Grant about a possible tour in New York.

"A tour? I don't know, Jake. I don't know if I will have time for it. Plus, my full-time job wouldn't give me that much time off without proper notice."

"Grant, the tour wouldn't start for another two months if we get the gig. You'll have plenty of time. The tour would only be for two months long and the pay for you would be enough for you to quit your communications job. But you don't have to answer right now, just think about it."

Jake left the conversation at that. They did, however, continue to discuss business as they ate. After about forty-five minutes of eating and talking, they brought their evening to an end. They shook hands and part ways. Grant now was en route to home, and Jake was going to meet up with Samantha.

After the dinner took place, Grant was even more sure of what he wants to do. Every time he meet up with Jake, he would attempt to gather information out of him about himself. He wants to know what Jake did to win over these women. He wants to know the best way to capture their hearts. He especially wants to know what Jake did to capture Samantha's heart. That was his winning hand. Grant was going to use the same moves that Jake had used to corral Samantha toward himself.

"We'll know by Sunday morning if the tour is ours. They like us a lot. They said they need an opening act, and we don't seem like a bad choice." Jake is excited.

"Was that their exact words? Yes, Jake, those were their exact words."

"Whoa! Okay, okay, one more question. If you had to put money on us getting the gig, how much would you be willing to bet the gig is ours?"

"Jake …"

"What Sam? I'm just saying …,"

"Okay, Jake, I'll play your game. What is the amount of cash I get?"

"Uhm, Uhm … 100k."

"Well then Jake, I would slide eighty thousand into the center of the table. Wait! Wait! I'm going for broke, baby. One hundred thousand all in!" Jake is extremely optimistic at this time. He tells the crew to go home and get some rest. Then he tells them to report back at 3 p.m. on Sunday. The crew agrees and leaves satisfied with today's efforts. Jake then gives Samantha a big hug and kiss. He says to her, "You, me, drinks, and satin sheets tonight!"

"Jake, I would love to, honey, but you know I have to go home and get ready for movie night with my sister."

"Oh yeah, that's okay. Looks like drinks are off for us tonight, but the sheets part is still happening."

Then Jake says, "I gotta find me a drinking buddy."

"Hey, Grant, Jessie you guys busy tonight?"

"Well, I have to go to my daughter's recital tomorrow so I can't party tonight, sorry, Jake."

"It's okay, Jessie. It is what it is."

"Guess that just leaves you and me, Grant."

"Uhm, I just recently jumped on the bandwagon."

"Nah, Really? Any chance you may wanna get off at the next stop? C'mon, Grant, this is a huge occasion! If we get this, it could possibly boost our business across America!"

"Okay, but what if we don't get it, that means I would have fallen off the wagon for nothing."

"Well, at least the drinks would have been free." They both laugh.

"Grant says how about I go with you but I won't drink. You can celebrate for the both of us?"

"Grant, my man, you got yourself a deal! Now meet me at my house. I have to shower and through my zoot suit on."

"Okay, boss, whatever you say," Grant says with a smile.

It took about twenty minutes for Grant to arrive at Jake's place. Surprisingly to Grant, he had beaten Jake there. Grant had approached the door, and was able to peek into the living room. He found it kinda strange for the door to be ajar while it's becoming darker outside. Grant knocks on the door and says, "Hello." He then cautiously walks in and looks around the house saying, "Hello." He continues to get no response.

Grant has been to Jake's house a few times before, so the beauty of the two-story floor plan didn't shock him. As Grant looks around the spacious house, someone on the second level of the house caught his eye. His immediate attention was drawn to the upstairs. There she was. Covered with only a towel on, Samantha's presence graces the hallway as she walks from the bathroom to her bedroom. She walks by, with her hair, dripping with water, and her body having a radiant glow. she passes under a dimly lit hallway light, whistling to herself. Grant couldn't help but stare.

Unbeknownst to Samantha that Grant was there, she continues to walk down her hallway until she enters her room. After she closes her bedroom door, Grant snaps out of his trance.

He then walks back to the front door to close it. He closes it loudly to make it seem as though he has just arrived. This time he yelled, "HELLO!" so that Samantha can hear him.

Grant hears her bedroom door open, and her soft voice responds, "Hello?"

"Yea, it's me, Grant!" Samantha then begins dressing inside of her room. She was surprised that Grant had arrived so soon.

Samantha then steps out the room in a t-shirt with her hair up in a ponytail. She begins to walk down the stairs.

She is infatuating Grant with every step as she walks down the stairs, just by the way she shifts her thighs, one after the other. Even though walking down the stairs is simple mathematics, Grant just like what her walk equals up to. Samantha reaches the floor and extends her body to Grant for a hug.

Grant gladly accepts. "So, why are you dressing down to go out tonight?"

"Out?"

"I'm not leaving, I'm about to sit my fat self on this couch and watch movies with my sister."

"There's two of you?" Samantha laughs. "Yes, and she's the evil one."

Samantha then begins to walk to the couch, she grabs the remote, and turns on the TV. She reaches for the phone and begins to dial her sister's phone number. At this moment, Jake walks into his house.

"Hey! How did you beat me here?"

"He knows the city," Samantha chimes in.

"You're funny boo-boo." Grant then answers Jake's question.

"Well, like she said I know the city."

"You must have got caught on the 15 freeway. I listen to news stations. I took the street and freeway combinations."

"You are smart, man. Grant, my friend, let me go get ready."

Jake starts to disrobe as he launches up the stairs into the bathroom. Samantha then tells Grant he can have himself some juice in the fridge if he wants.

Grant is heading toward the fridge. He hears Samantha curse out loud to herself.

"What's wrong, Samantha?"

"My sister just flaked on me."

"So that means no bonbon's and James Bond for the two of you, huh?"

"Right you are, Grant." Samantha plops down on the couch.

"Hey, girl, it's not too late. Come with us."

"I'm pretty sure we are going to have a blast."

"Instead of me pouring out my drink on the floor and pretending that I'm getting hammered, I'll just simply pass them to you." Samantha laughs then she replies back to Grant.

"You're funny. I'll be fine here alone. I knew I shoulda gotten that dog when I had the chance."

Now, Grant laughs. "Don't worry, you got Jake."

"Tell me about it. That's one dog that's tough to keep on his leash."

"He'll be fine, Samantha. He'll be with me."

"Well, if need be, yank that collar of his if you see him getting out of line," Samantha says with a serious voice. Grant picks up on her phraseology and answers back.

"Oh I will, don't worry."

Samantha rises off the couch and heads toward her bedroom. She asks Grant to do something for her as she continues to walk.

"Can you grab Jake's things from the kitchen counter and put them in his basket on the coffee table? That man swears I move his things just because he can't remember where he puts them."

"No problem, Samantha."

Grant sees Jake's loose cash, car keys, wallet, and cell phone lying on the kitchen counter. He puts his glass of juice down, and collects Jake's items. As Grant is walking over toward the coffee table, a great idea dawns him. He places all Jake's items in Jake's basket. All but Jake's cell. He takes that, and places it underneath the couch throw pillows. He then leaves the living room area. Jake then exits the bathroom and makes his way downstairs.

"Hey, where did Sam go? She went into you guys' room."

"Okay. Cool. Give me five minutes to throw something on and we outta here, buddy."

Grant replies, Don't worry, I'm still on the clock. Take your time." (They both laugh as Jake heads for his room)

Ten minutes go by and Jake comes out of his room in casual wear. Black dress shoes, white dress shirt and a V-neck sweater. He goes to his basket and grabs his stuff. He pats himself down as he looks for his phone. Grant hears Jake blame Samantha for the misplacement of his phone. All of a sudden, Grant chimes in, "Maybe you left your phone in the car."

"You know what, Grant I think I did."

Samantha comes out the room and says "You guys have fun."

"Oh we will," says Jake.

Jake steps away from the basket were he keeps his items. He then tells Grant that now is the time to go bid Sam "adieu" because they are heading out. Grant tells Samantha good night before he leaves out the door.

They leave the house, before Jake sits down in the driver's seat. Grant starts to talk to him about this potential New York deal. Jake gets excited over the topic and forgets about his phone. The two of them talk about their plan of action if the plan goes through. Grant tells Jake that he is still kind of "iffy" on whether he will make the trip or not. He says, "We'll see what happens, when it happens."

CHAPTER VI

UNSTABLE FOUNDATION

Jake had taken Grant to this new bar that he wants to go to called, "Pass out."

It's been on Jake's list as a "thing to do." The two of them walk in and find seats at the bar. Jake turns to Grant and says, "Let the drinking begin." Then he starts to order his choice of beverages.

As the night progresses, Jake becomes more loose, more open. Not totally committing to being drunk as of yet, but borderline flirting with that action. Grant begins to ask him question about his style, his charm, and most importantly how did he get all the women that he did. Grant is determined to pick Jake's brain, to learn his secrets. With Jake being on the verge of sobriety and drunkenness, he's answering Grant's questions.

Giving every detail that he could remember about so many games he played on women, Jake starts to laugh about some of the ways he won them over. Jake starts to explain to Grant his most well thought out, most romantic tactic that he's ever concocted. The story that Jake has begun to tell sounds familiar to Grant. It wasn't a pleasant familiar none the least. It was a familiar that Grant didn't want to relive again. Grant's mind tunes out Jake as he begins to reminisce.

(FLASHBACK)

"JULIA!" Grant shouts as he enters the front door.

"Yeah, baby."

"Well I took your car to the wash today."

"Aw, you're so sweet, Grant. What do I owe you?" Julia says in a seductive voice.

Grant pulls out the flatten rose and the faded card and drops it on the dining room table.

"You owe me an explanation!" Julia looks at the card and flower. She immediately knows where it came from. She then looks at Grant and turns her defensive side on.

"So we're going through each other's things now, are we?"

"I was vacuuming. I moved your book. The book fell, and this fell out."

Julia reaches for the card and rose. Grant moves it back out of her reach.

"Give me that stuff, Grant, it isn't yours!"

"It shouldn't be yours either! Who the HELL is THIS FROM? So you make a perfect pair with this rose, huh?"

Grant threw the rose and card at Julia. She grabs the items and then storms off into the other direction. Then she turns to Grant and says, "At least someone thought that I was as perfect as this rose!"

(FLASHBACK OVER)

Grant then awakens from his past thoughts of the argument with Julia, and he starts to focus more on what Jake is saying. Jake is still becoming more drunk with every drink that he sips. The alcohol allows him to continue on the subject of the rose.

"In all honesty, Grant, I don't even remember that girl's name. I just know I was leaving soon, and I had to make my move quick. Desperate times call for desperate measures." Jake begins to laugh as he orders on more drink. Grant just sits there looking at him, his heart burning with anger. His initial thought is to ram the shot glass down Jake's throat and call it a day, but he didn't want to deviate from his plan.

Filled with rage, Grant manages to maintain his emotions as he continues to leer at Jake. Grant takes one more sip of his non-alcoholic drink, and at that very moment of eye contact that Jake makes with Grant, Grant says, "You dirty bastard" in a stern unwavery voice. Then Grant removes himself from the bar to go to the restroom to cool off. On the way to the restroom, Grant bumps into a gorgeous brunette with a fitted blue dress on. She was making her way to the bar. Grant turns to look at her one more time and he notices that she positions herself to the right side of Jake. Grant then pays no more attention and continues to the restroom.

As Jake gathers himself, the brunette has her eye on him. She watches his every move for a couple of minutes. She then decides to make her move on Jake. She slides closer to Jake with an unopened bottle of alcohol, and says to him, "Gee, I was going to invite you to share this with me, but it looks like you've had more than enough to drink."

"Who me?" Jake looks around the room.

"Yeah, you!"

"Girl, I'm just getting started!"

Jake and the women began to converse for a few minutes. The women then says to Jake, "Oh, where are my manners. Here we are just talking away, and we don't even know either other's names. Hi, I'm Cindy." Jake then introduces himself to Cindy. They continue on with their conversation.

Grant walks out of the restroom and is heads in the direction of his seat at the bar. It is to the left of Jake, and is still unoccupied. The closer Grant gets to his seat, the more laughter and talking he hears from Cindy and Jake. Now Grant can tell that Cindy is into Jake by the way she continues to look at him. The way she smiles and laughs at his every comment. Cindy totally focuses on what Jake is saying and nothing is breaking her eye contact from him, according to how Grant is perceiving it.

Grant then reaches his chair, and asks the bartender for a glass of water. As he sits with his back towards Jake, he contemplates over a way to make this situation arch in his favor. With Jake being so infused in the conversation, he doesn't realize that Grant has come back and has taken his seat next to him.

Cindy then goes on to make her move on Jake. In mid-sentence, Cindy leans over and kisses Jake right on his lips. With that being done, the conversation grew quiet, which made Grant look in their direction to see what was now taking place. For a brief moment, Jake was stunned by the kiss. He is then intrigued to find out what more she would like to do. Jake clears his throat and picks up his beverage. He takes a sip of it, then he sit his cup down on the bar. The "thud" of the glass caught his attention as his glass hit the countertop. That split second of noise has made him redirect his eyes. He glances at the hand holding the glass. He focuses on his marriage ring. Jake began to shake his head slowly from left to right as he began to think about Samantha. Jake lifts up his left hand and exposes the ring to Cindy and begins to talk to her.

"Did you notice this before you kissed me?"

"Yeah, to be honest, but I don't have a problem with it if you don't. I'm not here to get a ring from you, I just want something else." Jake's eyes grew wide open; he knew what she was getting at.

At this time, Jake sobers up some. Enough to know what is happening to him right now. Jake pauses for a minute, he looks in Grant's direction and notices that Grant is carrying on a conversation with the bartender. Jake takes his thumb on his left hand and starts to roll his ring around his finger. He faces Cindy again and starts up more dialogue with her.

"If you, if we, would have met ten months ago, we wouldn't be sitting here. I guess I must be a changed man, if I turn you down at this moment. You came to me with all the moves I used on women, but I can't fall for them. I'm sorry Cindy, I'm taken."

"Jake, is she here? You just said yourself that we wouldn't be sitting here if this was ten months ago. Get back to that thinking and let's get out of here."

"I can't. No matter how much I would love to, and believe me, I would love to, I can't."

Even though Grant was talking to the bartender, he still keeps an attentive ear to Jake's talk with Cindy.

Cindy then extends her to Jake and says to him "You must have some special lady at home. Well … take care, Jake. If you ever need any marital counseling call me." She gives Jake her business card and walks away. Jake then examines the card back and front. He turns to Grant and says "Did you see that!"

"See what?" Grant asks, although he knew what has happened.

"Look at this card that this woman gave me. I don't believe it! She's a marriage counselor, and she tried to ruin my marriage." Jake laughs as he hands Grant the card. Grant says to Jake, "Wait! The lady in the blue dress gave this to you and she wants to give you something else! I'm buying you a drink, buddy! You stood up to the devil in the blue dress and won!" They both laugh. Grant slips the card into his pocket.

Grant then spots Cindy leaving the bar. As the bartender was making Jake another drink, Grant said, "Man I thought I was through with restroom duty tonight! I'll be back." Grant immediately gets up and heads in the direction of the restroom. He turns to see if Jake is watching him and when Grant notices Jake wasn't, he heads out of the bar doors.

When Grant steps outside, he observes Cindy talking on her cell. The way he hears her conversation, it seems as though she was talking to a female friend of hers about what just took place in the bar. Grant then takes out his phone and pretends to dial a number. He goes on to act as if he is holding a very important business conversation. He keeps it quiet enough not to disturb Cindy, but loud enough for her to get the gist of his fake discussion.

Grant now was trying to time the exit of his phone call perfectly with the ending of Cindy's. So he keeps talking about a bogus deal while listening in on any "exit" word that Cindy might use to wrap up her discourse. After two more minutes of Grant's bantering, he hears Cindy say the key phrase he was looking for. "Well, girl its getting really cold out here, I'm about to go home."

At that moment, Grant starts to act as if his battery was dying. He was portraying the character of a man who just lost his phone signal real well. A few more words exchange between Cindy and her female friend, and then Cindy hangs up after saying goodbye. Cindy was now on her way to her car, but Grant calls out to her before she made it six feet away from him. "Excuse me, miss?"

Cindy turns back around and replies "Yes?"

"I'm sorry to bother you, but my phone just died, and I need to know if my business partner got the go ahead on our project. If I don't get this commission, my wife is going to kill me. Can I pay you to use your phone? It'll be quick."

Cindy pauses for a minute and thinks about it. He said some key phrases to her that puts her at ease, like business deal and wife. She figures it would be a short call. she lets him use her phone. Grant thanks her and takes her phone. He immediately calls Jake's phone and let it ring twice. Then he hangs up. He then texted Jake's phone twice. The texts read:

Why are you not returning my call?

The other one read:

So after all this time, you're not speaking to me anymore? FINE THEN! Consider me DEAD to you, JAKE!

Grant then erases the texts and the phone number he dials and thanks the lady for her phone. Cindy then said to Grant "Sorry that you couldn't reach him." Grant replies, "It's okay when he receives my text he will know to e-mail me. I'll just go to FedEx Office and check my e-mails there. Thank you again, ma'am."

"My name is Cindy, and don't you owe me some money?" Cindy giggles as she made that comment. Grant replies, "Oh yeah!" then he pulls out a twenty-dollar bill and hands it to Cindy. "Once again, thank you, Cindy." Then they part ways.

Now as Samantha sits at home by herself, she pauses her movie to go and make some more popcorn. As she is in the kitchen popping her corn, she hears two faint chiming sounds coming from the direction on the couch. She stops what she is doing to go investigate the two chiming sounds she hears. Samantha picks up the couch pillow and discovers that Jake's phone is sitting there. She remembers before he left that he was over in that area searching for something. She picks up the phone and flips it open and sees one missed call. She views the number and doesn't recognize it. Samantha blows it off though. It's plenty of numbers in Jake's phone that she doesn't recognize. Before she closes his phone, she sees that he has two text messages from this unidentified number. She opens the first text and begins to read it.

At first thought, this text shocks her. Samantha's heart began to race with anxiety. She starts to tremble a little as she reads the text for a second time. Now, being overcome by curiosity, so fumbles through his texts until she runs into the second most recent one sent. After capturing the lines from the text into her memory, she drops the phone in shock and in disbelief. She begins to act belligerent, taking her anger out on the phone. Samantha steps on it until it cracks and breaks, then she picks up the bulk of the mangled phone and hurls it into the kitchen.

She storms over to her house phone and begins to dial her sister's number. She walks into her bedroom, hoping and praying that her sister answers because she is not sure of what to do.

Samantha waits at the other end of a ringing phone in tears. She feels as though the past Jake didn't leave. She feels that "he" lay dormant, until what he considers an opportune time presents itself.

Meanwhile, Grant then comes back into the bar. Jake hasn't noticed he stepped outside. Grant then says to Jake, "Hey, buddy, I think it's about time we go now."

"Aw, come on, you big party pooper," says Jake, "I'm just getting started."

"I was afraid you were gonna say that. Look, Jake, it's late, you're drunk and I'm sleepy. I'm the designated driver, and your limo is about to leave with or without you. Let's go, pal." Grant helps Jake to his feet. Jake begins to stumble but Grant catches him and aids him out of the bar and into the car. Jake crashes out in the backseat. As Grant was driving there was total silence in the automobile. No radio, no air conditioner, no Jake. Grant was left alone with his thoughts. Pondering if this initial plan had worked. Grant became more nervous as he got closer to Jake's house.

Grant could now see Jake's house from a distance. As tense as Grant was, he forces himself to keep his cool as he pulls in Jake's driveway.

He then gets out of the car and goes to the backseat to help Jake to his feet. Jake was half in and half out of it. He was talking "drunk talk" all the way up to the doors of his house. Grant takes Jake keys out of his pockets and opens the door. He then helps Jake step in. when Grant himself steps inside the house, he hears a "crunch noise" as his right foot landed almost flat on the kitchen floor. Grant picks up his foot and wonders what this piece of plastic is. The house seems pretty quiet, nothing is out of place. The movie is still paused. Jake then starts to walk further into the kitchen by himself. He focuses on the shattered object on the floor that seems to be leading a trail into the kitchen sink. With blurry vision, it looks as though Jake has found his phone. Jake then yells to Samantha, "Did you break my phone?" says Jake in his drunk voice.

Three seconds go by and Samantha comes storming out of the bedroom, She tells her sister that she will call her back, and then she abruptly hangs up the phone. She launches the house phone at Jake's head with enough force to injure him.

Jake's reflexes are slow, so he was unable to counter attack. Luckily Sam doesn't have good enough aim, so the phone skins Jake's ear and shatters to pieces on the kitchen's back wall. Jake is in shock. He's trying to gain composer, and he is questioning Samantha about what is wrong with her. Grant see's that Samantha is trying to get to Jake, he rushes in-front of Jake to separate the two of them.

"Move the hell out of my way Grant! (yells Sam) This has nothing to do with you!"

"I just can't let you beat down a defenseless drunk husband. I mean … just look at him! Look! He can barely stand on his own two feet and you want him to answer questions that you know he isn't capable enough to comprehend! Give him a break, Sam, for tonight!"

Through the pushing and reaching past Grant, Samantha was unable to get ahold of Jake. She then becomes tired, and gives up on her efforts to grapple Jake. Then she backs off Grant, looks him right in his eyes and says, "My NAME is SAMANTHA!" She walks away from the two of them gripping her hair and growling at the top of her lungs.

Grant then turns to Jake and slaps him softly in the face. "You gotta hurry up and sober up man. She's pissed at you. What did you do?"

Jake answers him as he searches for words. "I … I … . dunno? You were with me tonight, what did I do? I didn't do a chick, did I?"

"Well, Jake I did leave you alone for a little while. I might have bought you some time to re-coupe over the night. You better have your stuff together tomorrow morning because you, my friend, are going to be interrogated."

As frustrated and upset as Samantha was, she storms back into the living room with a pillow and a blanket. She throws it on the couch and says, "Goodnight, Jake!"

Samantha then gives Grant this cold hard stare. Grant replies, "Now, what did I do?"

Samantha then asked Grant can she speak with him outside. When they step outside, Samantha breaks down in tears in Grant's arms. She then begins to speak. "I don't know how I fell so hard for this guy. He's a jerk! He's never going to change!"

"In Jake's defense, Samantha, you never did tell him what he is guilty of." She takes a step back from Grant and wipes her eyes. "Well, he left his phone here tonight. It must have fallen out of his pocket somehow. It rang for a minute, then his message box pops up. It was saying that they are threw. He should consider her dead to him."

"How do you know that it was a woman?"

"I called, Grant, I didn't speak but the woman answered the phone."

"Samantha," Grant says, "you can't just go jumping to conclusions until you have the facts to back you up—this is all speculation."

Samantha continues to wipe her eyes, then she calms down a little and replies back to Grant, "Maybe you're right. Maybe it was just another business deal, Grant. I just don't want to get hurt again." Grant lifts Samantha's head up and says, 'I don't believe you will."

Grant lets her head go and gives her a soothing embrace. Her head lies on his chest and his hands rest on her lower back. Then she realizes they are linked for too long. She lifts her head and tells Grant, "Well, thank you for making me feel more at ease about all of this. I'm going to spare Jake's life tonight, but when I return from my meeting in New York in two days, we are most definitely going to have a discussion."

"I can understand that, Samantha. Just let him sober up some, then attack him. Take it from someone who has had their heart ripped out of them before. I wouldn't want anyone to feel the way that I felt. Goodnight, Samantha."

Grant thinks back to what Jake had told him in the restaurant. Jake had told Grant to "Never let his emotion or his heart get in the way. Say what you need to say and get it done. You have a goal to accomplish." This maneuver was hard for Grant to do, but he figures that he has gotten the ball rolling now, and it's too late to stop.

As Grant turns and walks away, Samantha calls out his name, "Grant." He answers as he is turning back around to face her, "Yes?" "If something unsettling did take place tonight or any other night that you were with Jake, you would tell me, wouldn't you?" Grant stumbles for words. "You just told me, Grant, that you wouldn't want to see anyone go through what you went through, right? Ain't I someone?"

"Look, I really don't want to get caught up in the middle of you guys' personal problems. I don't know, Samantha, sounds like you want me to become a spy on my boss, your husband. I don't know." Samantha begins to cry again but very lightly. "Okay, Grant, I guess, I understand. I wouldn't want you to break the guy code. You have a wonderful night, Grant." She says in a sarcastic voice as she slams the door. Grant calls her name twice very quickly. He finally gives up and leaves. As Samantha is walking into the living room, she looks into Jake's direction as he sleeps in his clothes on the couch, snoring out of control with his mouth open and drool pouring down his left cheek. She picks up a throw pillow and do just that. She throws it and hit Jake right in the face as he sleeps. Samantha then yells at him, "Shut the HELL UP!" She goes to her room and turns in for the night.

When morning finally approaches, Jake awakens to the sunlight streaming on his face. Samantha was in and out of the bedroom getting dressed to go to her business trip. Jake gets off the couch with a slight headache and heads for the restroom. He decides to use the one upstairs to stay out of Samantha's way. After Jake washes his face and take some aspirin, he heads downstairs to face the music, whatever the music was. Soon as Jake opens the door, Samantha is standing there. Jake is greeted with a hard slap to the face that caught him by surprise. Stunned by what has taken place, all that Jake seems to hear out of Samantha's mouth is blah! blah! blah! He is still hung over, and this slap he recieves did not help him sober up at all.

Jake backs up and extends his hands toward Samantha and tells her to calm down.

"Why should I calm down?"

"So that we can talk about this like adults?"

"Okay, Jake, last night, the phone call and text you received when you mistakenly left your phone here! Start explaining."

Jake then remembers seeing his phone broken last night.

"So did you break my phone?"

"Yes, the hell I did!"

"How can I defend myself when I can't even see what was supposedly sent to me?"

"I've seen it!"

"So if you needed to see it or change the meaning of the text, or shift the words, Jake, I'm not falling for it."

"It's nothing like that, baby. I have no interest in no one but you."

Samantha turns toward the stairway and begins to walk away from Jake. "I have a plane to catch." Jake rubs his face where Samantha slapped him and continues to talk to her as she is walking away. "Samantha! SAM! C'mon you're going to leave? Just like this! Okay, I had a few beers, but that's all!" The door slams as she walks out of the house. Jake looks at the clock in his room and realizes that it's 10:23 a.m. "Damn it! I'm late!" He runs into the bedroom and starts to dress. Fifteen minutes later, he bolts out the door and heads to his studio.

When Jake arrives, his dancers are listening to music, socializing, and talking on their phone. The studio gets real quiet when he enters through the doors.

"Good morning everyone, sorry, I'm late. Give me a few minutes to get situated then we will be ready to roll." Everyone in the studio went back to what they were doing as Jake went into his office. He figures that after work, he'll swing by the phone shop and pick himself up a new one. He puts his bag in a chair in his office corner and heads to his desk. He notices a box sitting on top of his desk. He approaches the box with curiosity. When he gets close enough to identify the box he sees that it was a new iPhone with a note on it. The note reads:

What's up, Jake. I upgraded my phone plan today and picked this one up for you (since you don't have a phone anymore) now you can step into the real world

Jake laughs and opens the box. He is still in awe about what he can do with this phone, but at the same time he remembers why he broke his last one. Jake then convinces himself that he will only use this one until he has time to go and get another phone that isn't a smart phone.

Two days pass by, and Jake is only receiving work-related text from Samantha. She seems to be ignoring his questions about them as a married couple. She texts Jake and tells him she will be home tonight, Knowing this, Jake goes out of his way to make a romantic dinner at home for the two of them. Later that evening as Jake is watching TV, he hears a car door slam. He jumps up in hopes that it is Samantha. Jake then becomes excited because it is. He cuts the music on, the TV off, and then he dims the lights. "It's time for some action," Jake says to himself.

Samantha walks in exhausted from the business trip and the flight. She is happy to be home. The romantic setting in the house catches her eye and puts a smile on her face. She finally focuses on the table with the meal that Jake has prepared for them. Jake gets up out of his chair and walks over toward Samantha. He takes her hand and kisses it gently. Then he removes her coat and takes her luggage. Jake then comes back to Samantha and leads her to her chair. He begins to explain to her what he prepared for them. Jake serves her and then prepares his own plate.

The next set of words that comes out of Jake's mouth was "I'm sorry." He begins to describe what happened that night to the best of his ability. Samantha soon after forgave him. She was still kinda "iffy" on the whole subject but she didn't have any tangible proof. So she decides to let it go. As they were eating, the meeting that Samantha had in New York had slipped Jake's mind. He was more interested in her heart being back in-line with his. The conversation between them was flowing smoothly, and Samantha finally decides to bring up the meeting.

"So are you going to ask me about the meeting?"

"Oh yeah, I totally forgot." Sam looks at him with a "I don't believe you look."

"No, really I was more concerned with you speaking to me again. The meeting was the last thing on my mind." Samantha's doubtful look now turns into a blushful expression. "Aw, really, Jake?"

"Sam, I love you. I need you. Dance Studio 3 wouldn't even exist without you." Samantha extends her hand over the table and Jake does the same. They hold hands at the center of the table as Samantha begins to talk about the meeting. Jake then blurts out, "Wait! Wait! No matter what they said, we are still going to be on top again."

"I'm so glad you feel like that Jake because … THEY WANT US!"

"What? Can you repeat that again?"

"They like our performances. They like what we do. They want to give us a two-month trial run."

"WOW! That is some good news!" Jake is super excited. He jumps up and runs over to Samantha, and begins to hug and kiss her. He pulls Samantha up to her feet and begins to lead her in a celebratory dance for a moment. She continues to give him more details on the deal. She says, they have to leave in two weeks to prepare for their first show. There first show is scheduled a month from now Jake. Finally stops dancing with Samantha. He takes a seat and then pulls out his phone. He was anxiously trying to get in contact with Grant. As Grant voice message box picks up, Jake leaves a message for him. While that was taking place, Samantha looks up from her meal and gets a glimpse of Jake's new phone.

Tilting her head to the side in curiosity, Samantha questions Jake about his new phone.

"So … when did you pick up that elegant piece of equipment?"

"What? My phone? Oh, yeah, you haven't seen it yet. Grant got it for me. It's the latest iPhone."

"Jake, I know what it is. Why did you go with that brand? Can I see it?"

"Yeah, you're not gonna break it, are you?

"Is there something that is stored in there that would make me break it?"

"No, but there wasn't anything in my old phone either, and you broke that one."

Samantha mumbles, "I beg to differ."

As Jake hands her his phone, Sam doesn't spend too much time admiring the phone, before she touches the screen to awaken it. The first thing that pops on the screen was "enter password."

"So Jake, what's the password?"

Jake thinks about it for a minute, then he begins to speak "4-8-9 … " he stops suddenly and says to Samantha, "Nah, we are not about to go through this. That look in your eyes right now is suggesting to me that you don't trust me. I'm not giving you the code until I see the trust back into your eyes."

"So you set up this romantic evening, this music, the food, your apologetic attitude, and now we are reverting back to your dishonesty?" Samantha drops the phone on the table. She stands up, grabs her car keys and purse, and heads for the door. Jake then yells, "C'mon, Sam, why are you doing this? Grant gave me the phone! I didn't even know I was getting it!" Samantha slams the door on her way out.

"Fine then! LEAVE! YOU'RE STILL NOT GETTING THE CODE!" Jake yells out that statement as Samantha takes off in her car.

Jake grabs his phone and goes into his bedroom angry and frustrated. The night was ruined.

CHAPTER VII

JULIA

A full week went by without any serious resolve between Jake and Samantha. Jake, through his stubbornness and pride, wouldn't let Samantha win this one. He figures the argument they had a week ago was started by her, so she should be the one to end it. Samantha was looking more into being comforted by Jake. She wanted him to prove that she was still the only one for him. Because his past is so checkered by women, she isn't backing down either. The house felt cold when they were in the same room. Only discussing business plans amongst each other. Something has to break or this house will not survive.

As Samantha leaves out, Jake calls out to her. "Hey! Before I forget to tell you, I'm hanging out with Grant this evening. I'm going to try and convince him to come to New York for at least a month. I really need him to be on the sound board." Samantha turns and faces Jake. She just gives a simple response. "Okay, have fun." Then she continues out the door.

Now Grant new that Jake and Samantha weren't really on speaking terms, and he was thinking about his next move. He also knew that Jake wants to hang out with him later on after he gets off from his communication job. He has no problem with that as well. Grant only felt a little remorseful over Jake and Samantha's situation because he knows what it feels like to be shut out from someone who you really care about in life. In Grant's case, not only the fact that Julia abandoned him, but Tim did as well. Ever since Grant blew up on Tim over a month ago, they haven't really been on good speaking terms. Just mostly "Hi and bye" type talk. Just the other day, Tim requested to be placed on another job site, and the supervisor followed through with that request. Grant starts to lose touch on certain events in Tim's life. He hears through mutual friends that Tim's girlfriend is pregnant. Filled with pride and hurt, Grant wouldn't go up to Tim to congratulate him if Tim doesn't come and announce it to him personally.

So now Grant feels even more alone and without a soul to confide in. All in all, he is determined to see this through to the end.

The day grew darker as the weather grew colder. Grant was at home waiting on Jake to show up. Jake arrives at 6:00 p.m. as promised. He is ready to give it one more shot at convincing Grant to come on the business trip. He was even going to offer him more money. Jake and Grant did not just talk about the business trip. They conversed about other topics and issues as well. They talk about relationships; they talk about sports and barbeque recipes too. When the night was coming to a close, Jake's offer to Grant to travel with them was still on the table. Grant glances at his watch, and notices that it was 11:36 p.m. He then responds to Jake, while stretching and yawning.

"Well, Jake, it's too late in the evening to come up with an answer, but it's also too early in the week to come up with an answer. Let me sleep on it. I'll have your answer in two days." Jake being totally exhausted mentally and physically, he just agrees with Grant. They shook hands and Jake leaves Grant's house to make his journey home.

The following day, Grant did his eight hours at his communication job, and he thought about the New York trip, but he knows that in the end he is going to say no. He just wants to look like he pondered the idea for two more days. With one more day to spare, Grant is sure that Jake would stop asking him and search out an alternate soundboard coordinator.

Grant is driving home in his car. His cell phone begins to ring. He looks at the caller I.D. and realizes it's Samantha calling. Grant answers the phone.

"Hello?"

"Hey, Grant! It's me, Samantha."

"I know it's you. I thought you wrote me off."

"Nah, not yet. Maybe later on but not now." Grant laughs and continues to talk with Samantha.

"So, Samantha … what's up."

"Oh uhm … this Friday coming up, will you be the one to pack the equipment if you don't come with us?"

"Well if I don't go, I can at least do that. You know how Jake is, always forgetting something."

"Yeah, tell me about it. So for him to be interrogating you for half of all yesterday, he doesn't look as if he persuaded you at all."

"Well, Samantha, he tried his best. I just got a lot going on right now. I need the money, but I have to handle something personal first before I start traveling."

"I understand, Grant. It would have been kinda nice to have you to talk to in case Jake flies off the deep end at one of these shows."

They both laugh as they continue in their conversation.

"So if you don't mind me asking, Grant, if you need the money that this part-time gig provides, why did you spend close to 4 hundred dollars on a phone for Jake?"

"What? Can you run that by me again?"

"Why did you get Jake such an expensive phone? That type of phone and phones just like it has been known to get Jake in trouble."

"Trouble?"

"Yeah, girl trouble."

"I just bought the phone that he gave me money to get. I don't know all about this trouble stuff."

"Hold on, Grant, now I'm confused. Did you buy Jake that phone?"

"Well, technically, with his money. The day after his phone was smashed, he asked me to go get him an iPhone. I was already headed down to the cell phone place for myself anyway. He didn't even give me enough for taxes, so I threw in the rest—"

"Wait, WAIT! He specifically asked and gave you money for that phone?" Grant starts to ease back from his phone as he says, "Nah, you wait. This sounds like you two have issues and you're trying to bring me in, I told you I am—" A cry for help came from Samantha's lips.

"Grant, please, things seem to be falling apart. All I want is a little help. Please." Grant could hear that Samantha's voice is becoming frustrated over the phone. He figures that now was the time to go all in, she is weak at this point and he sees room to capitalize on the situation.

Grant begins to speak to Samantha again. "Okay, okay. Please don't cry. Yes, Jake did give the money for the phone. I figured he didn't have time, so he wanted me to go for him. I'm sorry, Samantha." While still kinda choked up, Samantha pulls herself together slowly and begins to talk back.

"It's not your fault, Grant. He just wants a phone I couldn't get into easily. He has something to hide."

The conversation draws to a silence for a second or two. Then Grant asks Samantha a question.

"Hey, earlier you said Jake was with me all night interrogating me. What do you consider to be all night?"

Samantha is quiet at this time. She finally replies back to Grant with her interpretation of "all night."

"Well, I know he went to work, got off probably round 4:30 to5:00 p.m. I'm thinking he met up with you around 6:00 to 6:30 p.m. He got home after 11:00 p.m." At this time Grant is the one who is quiet. Samantha starts to question him on his silence.

Grant calmly takes a deep breath. He exhales, and then he frantically explains some things to Samantha.

"First off, if any of this somehow seems to circle itself back to me through Jake, I will deny it. I will deny, deny, deny, up until my grave, then five years after I'm buried. I don't think people should have their heart stomped on, and I'm only here to inform. I won't confront him or step forward. You will have to catch him 'red-handed' without linking any of your information to me. Is that clear?"

Now the pause came from the other end of the phone as Samantha listens to Grant's proposal. She then gathers her thoughts and answers his question.

"Yes, Grant, I understand."

"Okay, since we got that out the way, I'll tell you what I know for a fact. Now, I haven't seen him do anything wrong, I haven't caught him kissing, hugging, or anything else related to unfaithfulness, but on the other hand, some of his actions have been suspicious. He didn't arrive at my house at 6:00 or 6:30. He got here a little after 9:00 p.m. He did leave here a little after eleven though. Now, for the three hours before he showed up to my house, I couldn't explain his whereabouts."

Samantha listens intently to what Grant is telling her. Her voice is a bit shaky. It is soft enough to barely make out what she is saying. Grant could tell she is in pain. "I'm sorry for whatever I can apologize for to make you feel better."

With tears falling from her eyes, Samantha then tells Grant, "You don't need to apologize. You haven't done anything."

"Oh yes, I did. All men are jerks and I just happen to be born a man." Samantha laughs through her cries. "If in any way he is out there messing around, don't worry about it. The universe knows who is right for each other and who is not made to be together. You will walk away from this unscathed."

"Thanks for that, Grant."

"Even though you and I haven't spoken in almost two weeks, those few words just spoken outweigh Jake's right now."

"Wow you've rendered me speechless now, Samantha."

"You can call me Sam, Grant. You can call me Sam." After that comment, Grant feels confident in the way this is turning out. Samantha then tells Grant that she has to go now. She has some things to think about. Grant then tells her that he understands and would let her go now. They both say their goodbyes, but before Grant gets off the phone, he tells her that he would send the equipment off Friday. Grant assures her that she would have it by close of business day Monday. She joyfully thanks him, and they hang up their phones.

Grant places his cell phone in his cup holder and continues to drive. His phone begins to ring again. The ringing excites him because he thinks it's Sam calling back, but it's his Boss. This time Grant secures his Bluetooth in his ear, and then he and Steven begin to speak.

"Hey, what's up, Steven?"

"Weren't you and Tim on the Culture Project together up until a few days ago?"

"Yeah, Steve, that is correct."

"Tell me something: which one of you guys did the ordering for supplies last week? The name on the invoice is unreadable."

"Was there a problem with the ordering, Steve?"

"You damn right there was! Too much of it! That project has already lost us a lot of profits with labor, but one of you guys went over the budget with the supplies! We are already laying people off, and when we have to double up on foremen and send two on the same job, it kills our profits even more and you know it! I'm putting all my money on Tim. He's done it before—twice! If it turns out to be him, it's not going to be a bright future for him here. I just want to give him the benefit of the doubt and call the both of you."

Grant drives in silence over Steve's rant. Not only is he trying to stay focused on the road while driving, he is also now put into a situation involving his closest friend. Even though Tim and Grant have not spoken for a while, that doesn't mean that he wishes ill will to his comrade. Tim has much more to lose at this point in life. Grant understands what he has to do.

"Steve, I thought since it had been a week or so since that order, all was forgotten. I guess I was wrong. I placed that order. I was being bombarded with problems, plus my own life isn't of trophy quality either. I'm sorry, Steve. I dropped the ball."

"You? You Grant, dropped the ball? You wouldn't happen to be covering for Tim now would you? Let me just tell you the consequences of your actions if you are covering for him. This is no light matter because of the money that was lost. There will be suspension, probably even termination depending on Mark's mood. Oh, and speaking of Mark, do you know where he is right now?"

"No I don't, Steve."

"Well our boss is in Minnesota searching out some real estate for him and his wife. See what else you don't know, Grant, is that Mark is gonna retire way sooner than later. When he steps down in a few months, I move up. He doesn't want to run the business from Minnesota. He wants me to do it. When I step up, what do you know, my position is now vacant. Grant, do you know that Mark himself mentioned you for my position. If you were the one that placed this order, I think that deal is gone. So let me get this clear one last time. . . did you complete and sign off on this order?"

As Grant comes to a complete stop at a red light, he ponders about the answer that will alter his professional life for good. He really doesn't want to take the heat for something he didn't do especially now that he was provided this information. Right before he began to speak, an image of his friend Tim came into his head. There stood Tim, haunting Grant's memory of things to come of him and his new family if he backs out now. Grant takes a breath, releases, then begins to utter the sentence. "Like I said earlier, I made a mistake."

"Well, Grant from what you are telling me, it possibly could be a grave mistake. Continue to go to your worksite for the rest of the week. Mark will be back on Monday. Come down to the office Monday morning." Steve hangs up.

Grant takes the Bluetooth out of his ear in dejection. The car behind Grant horn blows to alert Grant to make his left turn with a freshly green arrow lit, Grant presses on the gas pedal. With Grant still being in distraught, he isn't aware of the car barreling down the adjacent intersection, desperately trying to make a yellow light that has already expired. The next thing that Grant encounters is the car headed straight for him with its horn blaring! Automatically Grant's foot smashes on the gas pedal, increasing his speed, throwing his body back farther into his seat. The speeding car misses Grant's driver's door and plows into the rear of the driver's side. This sends Grant's car spiraling out of control. He comes to a complete stop right side up against a traffic pole light. After Grant's airbags deflate, he looks around at the wreckage and notices the destruction that is now before him on the block. He glances over at the other car and sees the driver shaken up pretty badly. Grant then feels moisture on his forehead. He touches the area on his head in question and looks at his hand. Grant discovers that his hand is covered in blood, he blacks out.

(The next day…)

As she sleeps, her eyes are wondering. Rapidly moving back and forth underneath her eyelids, Julia is powerless to wake up. She wants to be out of this hellish dream that is taking place in her mind. Her phone begins to ring, and she awakens from her nightmare with a ghastly scream. She looks around the room in disarray for her phone. She pounces up off the couch and sees her phone on the kitchen table, and goes to answer it. "Hello?"

"Hey, Julia, it's me Carol." Still trying to adjust from sleep mode, Julia takes a little time to collect herself. She begins to respond back to Carol.

"Hey, how are you doing?"

"I'm doing just fine Julia, just fine."

"That's good to hear, Carol. So is your baby shaping you to be the size of a house?"

"I am getting bigger. Tim says he likes me like this. He says a little more meat never hurts anyone." Both chuckle at Carol's comment. Carol then begins to talk seriously with Julia.

"Hey, Julia, I have something to tell you."

"What is it?"

"It's about Grant." Julia starts to become hysterical at this time, recalling in her mind the nightmare that she just escaped from. The thought that holds her captive now seems to playing out in real life. She mumbles out loud, "I just seen it in a dream, he's dead … Oh my god! HE'S DEAD!" Carol quickly jumps in and begins to speak.

"Julia! Julia!" she yells. "He's not dead! Calm down, Julia Please!"

Julia finally calms down and asks Carol to explain to her what happened. Carol explains to her what the doctor explained to Tim. Carol explains as Tim was put down as an emergency contact, that's how he was reached. She tells Julia that Grant is in a coma at St. John Memorial. It seems as though Grant has a herniated disc in his lumbar area. Other than that, no more serious injuries have been detected." Julia jumps in and says, "Okay, let me get this straight, St. John Memorial, right?"

"Yes, Julia."

"Okay, I'm on my way." After Julia says that, she hangs up the phone, grabs her purse, car keys, and jacket, and heads out the door. She decides to drive to the train station and ride the train into the city. She has too much on her mind to be driving for 3 ½ straight hours.

The drive to the train station was tense for Julia. No radio, only the noise of her thoughts running through her head. As the sun is still rising on this dense foggy morning, the only thing that drowns out Julia's thoughts, are the sounds of the windshield wipers on low to wipe off some of the mist that the fog has brought in. In Julia's mind, she really doesn't know what she was doing. All she knows is that she must do it.

She arrives at the station and parks her car. She then begins to sprint to the ticket booth. Just her luck the first train leaving for the city leaves in thirty minutes. Julia frantically dumps her purse out onto the ticket counter to search for her credit card. After being handed her ticket, she gathers her belongings and heads to the train terminal where she is departing from. As she sits in the terminal, she begins to finally cry silently about Grant's present situation. The more she recollects on their marriage, the more tears come flowing from her heart. Julia is so heavily into her emotions that she doesn't recognize that her train is boarding. She finally looks up and sees the boarding procedures in effect, so she gathers her belongings and goes to stand in the short line.

Julia gets a window seat away from everyone else. She sits quietly until the train takes off from the station. She looks out the window for comfort, but none is to be found. The mist on the window, the chill factor in the air kills her chances of a beautiful day out. Julia then takes her index finger and begans to draw on the misty window. She draws a heart. The letter J is placed above and to finish it off, she drew a diagonal arrow right through the center of the heart. Julia then lays her head up against the cold glass window and began to fall asleep underneath her jacket. She could remember happier times with Grant before Jake was ever part of the picture.

(FLASHBACK)

Julia has set up a surprise date for Grant. He agrees to go with her anywhere, except to an opera. Grant was real familiar with the area that Julia takes him to on this particular time, but he doesn't know which place she has in mind for them. As they got out of the car, Grant turns to Julia and says, "Well, at least it's not the opera." Julia laughs and says, "I remember the rules." Julia then walks over to Grant who starts to put up some resistance. Julia says while laughing. "You said no opera." And Grant responds back, "Yeah, but this is not fair. This is like the opera in a frame." They both laugh as Grant gives in and continues to move forward with Julia. They continue to walk until they reach the entrance of the art gallery. Grant grabs Julia by the hand and holds it tight. Before they proceed in, he began to hum the theme to the "Twilight Zone" series. Right after he stops humming, he says to Julia, "Now you are about to enter, the twilight zone." Julia starts to laugh uncontrollably as they proceed into the art gallery.

(FLASHBACK OVER)

Her eyes are now beginning to get heavier and heavier as she reminisces about this fond memory of her and Grant. She struggles to fight the slumber bug off a little more, so her memories can continue to play out as before. Shortly thereafter, she dozes off. Julia's dream world began where her memory ceases. Grant and Julia are discussing one painting that makes no sense at all to Grant. Julia sees that Grant is getting himself worked up over the conversation, so she began to move on to the next painting. When she gets about 300 feet from Grant, she turns around and says to him, "Hey, baby, let's go look at that one." Grant doesn't even acknowledge her. He continues to stare at the picture that he just doesn't quite get. He places his hand on his chin and begins to rub it. Then he starts to take steps toward the picture.

Julia senses that he's unhappy with something, and she calls out to him.

"Grant! What are you about to do?" in a hushed voice. Grant says nothing. He grabs the picture, one hand on each side. He starts to shake it vigorously. Julia then becomes louder. "Grant! What the hell are you doing? You're going to get us in trouble." Grant manages to rip the picture off the wall and he says to Julia in an irate voice.

"I get this pictures meaning now! It's about love … " As Grant continues to talk, he smashes the picture against the ground with intentions on breaking it into pieces. Grant now has the attention of the browsers in the gallery. "This picture represents love, Julia! Something that we don't have, Julia! Something that we had! Something that you let slip away!" Julia now raises her voice.

"What the hell, Grant! Why are you doing this?"

"NO! NO! Julia! The question is where are you going?" He looks Julia square in the eyes. "I don't want to see you! Don't come here, Julia! You left me. Just stay gone!" Julia wakes up in panic. She looks around the train's cabin. People are reading, some are eating, others conversing with one another. Julia takes a deep breath to calm herself down. She looks at the window where she drew the heart with Grant and her initials. The condensation had broken the heart down the middle. Julia takes that as a sign.

The ringing of Julia's phone startles her even more. On the other end was Tim with some good news about Grant. "Hey, Julia!"

"Hey, Tim you scared me. Well, not you, literally the phone call did."

"Are you ready for some good news Julia?" she pauses for a moment, then she continues to talk to Tim.

"Yea, I guess so."

"He's awake!"

"What?"

"He is awake!"

"I'm here at the hospital now. I was just visiting him, talking to him. while I was looking away, I felt something grab my hand. I looked back in his direction and he was staring me right in my eyes with his! Isn't this great news or what?"

Julia starts to fumble for words to say in response to Tim.

"Well, yeah, I'm happy, he's recovering well."

"So how long till you arrive here, Julia?"

"How did you know I was on my way?"

"Carol told me."

Julia starts to get enraged. "Well, I'm not!"

"You're not? But—"

Julia cuts in. "It doesn't matter what Carol thought. I'm not coming to the hospital."

"What's gotten into you, Julia??"

"Life. Me moving on. That's what has gotten into me. Now, I'm happy he is awake. I really am, but I can't see him right now. Not right now."

"If not now, when Julia … when?" Once again Julia takes a pause to think about her answer. Her hardcore demeanor began to break down as she begins to talk to Tim again. While on the verge of tears, she manages to hold it together to talk with strength and composure.

"Look, Tim, I am on a train. I am on my way to see Grant. I do need to see for myself that he is all right, but I just can't go through with it now."

"It will be all right, Julia. I will wait here until you come. We'll do this together. All you need to do is hear his voice. Let me go back in the room and put him on . . . "

Once again, Julia cuts in. No, Tim! Don't go in that room. Don't tell him that you spoke to me. I'm not ready!" Julia begins to cry. "Why don't you understand? I am not ready. Now, keep my number, call me from time to time, let me know how he is doing, but don't try and make me come and see him. When I'm ready, I will come, but right now, I'm in pieces." Julia wipes her eyes as the phone grows silent after her comments.

Finally, Tim says in a sullen voice, "Okay Julia, okay. He won't know we've spoken. You have my word. Carol and I miss you and I know Grant does too." With that being said, Julia said her goodbyes to Tim and they both hang up there phones.

Tim stays in the hallway a little while longer to gather his thoughts and to get back to a cheerful attitude. He then glances in Grant's room through the glass on Grant's door. He sees Grant talking to his doctor. Grant then turns his head, and catches Tim looking inside the room. Tim then takes a deep breath, puts on a smile, and opens the door and walks into the room. With a faint voice, Grant begins to speak.

"Hey, buddy, nice to see you here."

"Well, it's nice to see you at all," says Grant.

"Tell me about it. I guess the universe has a way of working things out between friends, huh?"

"You couldn't be more right, Tim. So how is Carol coming along?"

"She's great, Grant. I get the feeling that this kid is gonna be special. What about your other one?" They both laugh. "Well you know what I mean, Grant, and thanks to you, their daddy will still have a job to provide for them."

At the end of that sentence, Tim began to cry. His emotional side comes to life as he expresses gratitude for what Grant did for him.

"I mean, Grant, you could've told the truth. You could've told Steve that it was me, but you didn't. We were still not on good speaking terms and you had my back. How can I repay that?" Tim then, leans in and gives Grant a hug while he is sobbing.

Grant yells "Ouch! Ouch! Be careful, buddy, my back ain't right yet." Tim lifts up and apologizes.

Grant then sits himself up in the bed and speaks.

"Well, if I were in your shoes, and you were in mine, I know you would have done the same for me. Look, Tim, I know it's been a couple of months that we haven't really talked. I've been a bitter drunk friend on the verge of breakdown.

"The only thing you wanted to do is help. I'm sorry for pushing you away. I should have let you help me."

"It's not too late, Grant. I'm still right here for you, buddy."

"That's good to know, Tim, because until I have this surgery, I'm going to need your help. Like I said Grant you got it."

Tim's cell rings. He answers it and begins to hold a conversation with Carol. She reminds him of the doctor's appointment, and he tells Grant that he has to leave now. Grant calls Tim to get his attention.

"Hey, Tim?" Tim tells Carol to hold on and he answers Grant.

"Yeah, man," Grant reluctantly asks Tim.

"Have you heard from Julia?" Not willing to break his word with Julia, or break Grant's heart all over again, he decides not to tell him about his conversation with her.

So Tim clears his throat and looks down at the floor, and tells Grant, "No man. I haven't heard from her in months. My new phone erased her number."

Grant begins to play it off as though he is not hurt. He tells Tim that maybe it's for the best they didn't know where she is. Maybe now, he can start over. Maybe this accident is supposed to close the last chapter in this book so he can start anew.

Even though Tim understands every word that Grant has said, he just doesn't believe that it is really over in Grant's heart. Once again, Tim says his goodbyes and departs from the room. At this time, Grant just sit up in his bed, thinking of all that he has done and what he plans on doing. He asks himself, Is it worth it? to make someone hurt the way I had hurt? He sits in his hospital room and ponders on that question until he falls asleep.

Now Julia has one of two choices to make. Even though she clearly takes her stance on visiting Grant, she is contemplating on whether she will allow her body to overturn a call her heart has made. With her final stop approaching, she is really torn between unboarding here, and making her way home, or staying on the train until her destination is complete. She knows that if she takes plan B, there would be no turning back. She will have to face emotions she has buried, relive some hurts forgotten, and possibly set herself up for pain in the future.

As the train pulls into the station, it has a lay over time of three minutes. Julia stands up and thinks to herself, That's not enough time. Why does every decision in my life have to be rushed? Julia takes all her belongings and steps off the train. She paces back and forth on the platform. She doesn't care what people are thinking about her. She doesn't care what they say. She just knows that she wants to get this decision right. The conductor says over the loud speaker "Doors will be closing in one minute." Julia grabs her things and heads back to the train. She glances up at the seat where she has sat previously. The drawing on the window still stands. It is that drawing that crushes her spirits. She slowly backs away from the train, and then she turns away from the train and begins to walk. She hears the train doors close. Then she hears the train depart.

CHAPTER VIII

CONSUMMATE

The world around Grant is peaceful this weekend. As he lies in the hospital bed recuperating from his injuries, he makes no phone calls, nor does he answer any. He knows that life would soon have to operate for him again, but he tries to hold on to this silence and serenity for as long as he can.

It is Monday night. Grant knows that he missed two important things this Monday. The shipping of the music equipment, and his meeting with Steve and Mark about his job. Grant figures that since he and Tim were good again, that Tim would shed light on his present condition. The only thing he doesn't want to deal with is the music equipment. In his two days of deep concentration, he decides not to go through with his plan. Maybe the accident was a sign. Maybe he has caused enough damage in their relationship. His new plan is to let it all go focus on getting himself together, and letting the McKhals fade out of his life. Grant knew that thought was easier said than done.

Grant awakens to the voices of doctors standing over him evaluating his condition. They all seem to be in agreement that he can leave. Since Grant decides not to have the surgery on his back just yet, the medical staff tells him that he will be released later this afternoon. They suggest that he calls a cab or call someone for a ride home, because the meds haven't completely worn off yet. Grant agrees. He wants to see the outcome of his actions. To Grant's dismay, Steve actually doesn't drop the "iron fist" on him, because he can't. Mark will not let him. When Mark finds out about the accident, he tells Steve to give Grant an extra month off.

As much as Steve opposes Mark's decision, he breaks the news to Grant. Steve could not manage to get off the phone without letting Grant know that this doesn't mean that he's off the hook. Steve's exact words to Grant were: "You're still fish bait. The small fish nibbles, but when he runs the ocean, the bait is going to get eaten." Grant took a deep breath and said back in response to Steven, "You do what you got to do, little fish. Until then, I'll just keep wiggling." Steve came back with a sarcastic "whatever" and hans up the phone.

About six hours passes and Grant is eager to go. He's been lying in the hospital bed for about a week, and to top it off, he has a craving for some good food. Dr. Hershel walks into the room to ask Grant if his ride is on the way." Grant knows he didn't call anyone for a ride, so he tells the doctor that he is going to catch a cab. The doctor nods in agreement and begans to leave the room.

Just as the doctor is leaving, the nurse opens Grant's room door and says, "Mr. Richards, your ride is here." Grant has no clue of who might be walking through that door to pick him up. Grant is thinking to himself, What ride?

Samantha walks into the room with an irate look upon her face. She sternly looks Grant in his eyes and says, "Hello, Grant. I'll give you the benefit of the doubt for four days. I started to worry about you Monday when my package didn't arrive. I stopped calling you because I was coming back to California Tuesday morning. I was going to pick up my equipment myself. For some strange reason, I start to check hospitals and jails and your name came up here. Now I say I gave you the benefit of the doubt for four days. This is the fifth day. They say that you were responsive yesterday. No call, Grant?

No text? No anything?" Grant is clueless on what to say. The doctor and nurse began to ease out of the room as Samantha stares Grant down. Then he begins to form sentences.

"I … .I … . uhm, I didn't know what to say. I didn't want you guys to worry."

"Worry? Worry? You guys? Look don't take offence, but Jake is so caught up in the production out in New York, the only thing that he noticed missing is the equipment."

Grant gives a little chuckle and says, "Wow, I'm that missed, huh?"

"Well, if it at all makes you happy, I was a little concerned for your well-being. Then I started to think that you stole our equipment." They both shared in on the laughter.

As Grant is gathering his belongings, he turns to Samantha and asks, "So what made you come to the hospital?" Samantha looks at Grant as though he just asked a senseless question. She then says to Grant, "Well, I've come to see if you really did steal the equipment." Grant then begans to laugh out loud as he packs his bag. All of a sudden his laugh is cut short. A sharp pain runs up his back and temporarily weakens his movements. He places both his hands on the hospital bed and waits a few seconds until the pain subsides.

"What's wrong, Grant? Do you want me to call the doctor?"

"No, I'll be fine. It's just my back. I guess this pain will come and go until I have the surgery."

"When are you going under the knife then?"

"I'm not, I'm scared of needles, knives, doctors and clowns." Sam laughs.

Grant continues to talk. "I'll see how long I can take this pain. Maybe it will heal itself. The body is an amazing specimen."

"So do you think you can drive yourself to your place if need be?"

"Good question. I don't know the answer to that yet."

"Well, do you need a ride now?"

"I was going to catch a cab, but if you're going my way, I'm not turning you down."

"Okay then, Grant, I'll go get a wheelchair so we can wheel you out of here, buddy." Grant sits on the bed and says, "Thank you."

Samantha says, "No prob, you'd do the same for me." Sam gets quiet for a second after the response. "He wouldn't be there for me."

"Why do you say that, Sam?"

"It has happened before and I doubt it would not happen again."

After Samantha said that, she repeats to Grant her arrangement to get the wheelchair from the hall. Once again Grant said, "Thank you, this means a lot."

Samantha helps Grant into her car. She then closes his door and starts to head over to her driver's seat. The first few minutes of the car ride were quiet, and kind of uncomfortable for Grant. He hid his back pain as best as he could. The doctor has given him a month's prescription of pain killers and he thinks to himself, These will be gone in a week.

Samantha interrupts his meditation and starts conversing with him. "So … did you like the hospital food?"

"I grew fond of it. I grew so fond of it, that I'm contemplating re-injuring myself just so I can have another week's helping of meatloaf." Sam burst out into laughter.

She began to fan herself while laughing and driving. Then from a joyful moment, comes tears of abandonment felt by Sam. "What's wrong, Sam? I didn't mean to make you cry. It was a joke. I guess it is a really bad one at that." Samantha continues to fan herself while driving. Through her laughter, she says to Grant, "It's not that it is a bad joke, it's just the fact it was a joke. I don't mean to dump all my problems on you every time I see you, but I have no one else to talk to." She stops laughing and starts to cry more, but she continues to speak. "Ever since we got this big contract, Jake has changed more than ever. It's just 'hi and bye,' we rarely go out anywhere without being on speaker phone or on a conference call. We don't even have any alone time because he is busy going over numbers." Grant doesn't know what to say or how to respond. He reaches down by the center console and places his hand on top of hers. He then caresses her hand gently and says, "Everything will work itself out, you'll see. You will see."

For the next five minutes, they continue to ride in silence as they draw nearer to Grant's home. When they pull up to the door, Grant breathes a sigh of relief that he's finally home. As he turns to tell Samantha, "Thank you." He notices she shuts her car off and unbuckles her seatbelt.

"Uhm, you don't have to help me any further, I can handle it from here." Samantha looks at Grant and says, "I don't know who you think you're fooling, but you are in some pain, my dear. Your facial expression fifteen minutes ago gave it away. I'm figuring those pain killers are only going to last you a week."

"I'm going to try and make them last longer." Grant begins to laugh as he turns and exits the car. When he stands up, he feels a sharp pain throughout his spine. He whines for Sam's help.

"See, I told you. Just like a man, once you guys see blood, you call out for mommy."

They both laugh as Samantha helps him out of the car and into his house.

She helps Grant down onto the couch and she immediately goes into the kitchen. She starts to rummage through his cabinets. "Grant, do you have any tea?" As Grant starts to relax a little bit, he says, "Check the top left cabinet, second shelf."

"Okay, I got it. This should help you relax a little better." As the tea is brewing, Samantha and Grant go on to converse. They have great conversations over their cups of tea. Grant thinks it feels real good, real natural to sit on the opposite side of a table from a woman and talk, and for the first time in a long time, he smiles on the inside.

Time slowly creeps up on the two as they learn about each other. Samantha's phone begins to ring while it sits in her purse. There first reaction is to stop talking so they could find the location of the phone, then Samantha laughs as she goes to retrieve it from her purse. By the time she reaches her purse, the phone has stopped ringing, and a "New voice message" was left. From the expression on her face, Grant figures that it must have been Jake.

"Samantha, is everything okay?"

"Yea, Grant everything is fine. He's probably just calling to check up on me and to ask why I haven't been to the studio yet."

"Is he still mad at me for not going to New York?"

"He didn't mention anything when I left, more than likely, he doesn't even know that you were in an accident." Grant has a surprised look upon his face.

"Well, you can chalk that misinformation up to me. I should have told you, guys."

"Don't worry about it Grant. I know that with this New York gig happening, he's not going to dwell on the news too long. He'll just be happy that you're okay and that the equipment is in our possession." Once again they laugh.

Grant responds, "You're just not going to let that one go, huh?"

"Nope, it's my running joke of the day. Hey look, I have to be going now.

"I guess I should go do my job at the studio while Jake is away. Call me, Grant if you need anything. I'm flying back to New York Friday night, then I will be back here Sunday night."

"What about Jake? Is he coming?"

"Nah, for these next two months he will be occupied by work, as usual. I doubt if he even makes one trip here. This is what he is sending me here for."

Grant nods his head in agreement. "Oh, okay, that sounds cool." As Samantha is walking toward the door, she turns back into Grant's direction and walks toward him with her arms stretched out wide. This gesture shocks Grant, but neverthe-less, he doesn't let a chance for a quick embrace from Samantha pass him by. She then heads to the door and leaves Grant on the couch. Grant was somewhat clueless on where to start. He turns the TV on and glances into his bedroom. He notices that he hasn't done laundry in a while, He thinks to himself, before he dozes off, "That's what I'll do, I'll go washing."

Bright and early, after Grant prepares himself for the day, he dresses in the only clothes that he has left that are clean. He puts on his gray sweatpants with a size small pink shirt that he had bleached during an earlier wash. He figures, What the hell, I'm going to the wash house, not a night club. Grant calls Sam to see if she is available to take him. When Sam answers, she is happy to hear from him "Hello, Grant! Are you okay?"

"Yeah, I'm fine, Sam, thanks for asking. Hey … about that 'If you need anything,' I have one of those moments right now."

Sam giggles then begins to speak. "So what is this 'anything' that you need help with?"

"My clothes, I need them washed."

"Honey, I don't wash just anyone's underwear."

Grant laughs and says, "No, not like that. I mean, can you take me to the wash house down the street?"

"Don't you have a washer/dryer set at your house? It is the new May Tag, right?"

Grant looks at his washer and dryer set up and quickly says, "I don't know where my mind was at. Probably it is on my back. The set up did run awesome when it was working. Now, when I turn the washer on, after the first cycle, it decides that it doesn't want to hold the water anymore. I think I almost drowned the last time I used it."

Samantha giggles. "Okay, give me until noon. I have to get the studio in order. I should be over before 12:30 p.m."

"Sounds like a plan to me." Grant and Sam say their good-byes and hang up.

As Grant gathers his clothing that he is going to wash, he empties his pants' pockets and organizes the clothes by color to the best of his ability. He places his hand into the right front pocket of the pants he wore to the bar with Jake that one night and pulls out the marriage counselor's card. Grant flips the card over back and forth, and back and forth as he ponders on an idea. Nothing comes to his head at that time. Grant decides to stick the card in the dresser mirror just in case he may need her services.

Grant is awaken from his nap by the sound of his doorbell ringing and ringing and ringing. He checks his watch, and it was 2:47 p.m. He begans to walk to the door.

"Who is it?"

"It's Sam." Grant opens the door then he looks at her watch. She playfully pushes him back and says, "I had to go home and gather some of my things too. Kill two birds with one stone, right?" Grant laughs at her comments. Then he agrees with her. Sam begins to walk back to the car and Grant yells, "Hey, since my back's being all tweaked and stuff, can you take my loads?" Sam starts to blush and says to Grant in a playful voice, "Excuuuuse me?" Now Grant laughs. "You know what I mean. My clothes, girl, you knew what I meant … my clothes."

"Well … since you clarified that, just point me to the sack and I'll take it." With a smirk on Grant's face, he cocks his head a little to the left, then rubs on his chin as though he was in thought. He straightens out his head, and then he points to the bedroom, "My clothes sack is on my bed. If you don't have a problem with going in there, you should be fine." Sam smiles at Grant and proceeds into his bedroom to carry his dirty laundry out to the car. As Grant waits on Samantha to return, some thoughts run through his mind. Then he turns away from his room and starts to make his way to the car.

He positions himself in the car slowly. He takes one of his pain pills and watches as Sam walks down the stairs with his clothes. She opens the back door and places Grant's clothes next to hers and Jake's clothes in the backseat. She closes the cars back door, and Grant's clothes begin to lean to the left on top of Sam's clothing. Samantha finally gets into the car and begins to pull off. The first thing Samantha ask Grant when she pulls off is, "So if you don't mind me asking, what went wrong in your marriage?"

Grant begins to recline his chair back to make himself more comfortable. He turns away from Samantha and faces the passenger's side window. At that point, he is not ignoring her question, just pondering on how to answer her question. Samantha then says to Grant, "Okaaay, change of subject. I guess we are not ready to discuss that yet. I understand." Grant then turns and faces Samantha. "It's not that I am not ready. It's just that I feel this is going to be a happy day. I don't want to ruin it by bringing up sad, depressing things. I will say that I … Grant Richards was not always a good loving, listening husband, but I was faithful. I was there for her. I tried. I guess, trying don't get things done. I can say with every bone in my body that I loved that woman. She eventually stopped caring for me and left. With her departure, she took my heart. That's all I can say about that."

The car grows silent after that is said. Samantha doesn't really know what to say. She is speechless.

Samantha clears her throat and begins to talk to Grant. "So I know this is a stupid question, but you ever find out who the guy is?"

Grant turns his head into Samantha's direction. For a split second, she takes her eyes off the road to make eye contact with Grant. With a stern look upon Grant's face, his answer was a solid, "Yes, I know the identity of the man who slept with my wife."

Samantha quickly focuses her attention back on the road. She feels as though Grant has given her the coldest stare one human can give another human. Grant now turns himself away from Samantha's direction, and continues to look out of the window.

With more silence taking over the car, Samantha then asks Grant, "So … what did you do to the guy when you saw him?" Grant continues to look out of the window as he answers Sam.

"Nothing. I did nothing to him, at least not yet."

"I don't think I should ask you anymore questions. Grant, I don't want to end up being an accessory to a murder." Samantha laughs as Grant gives a smirkish gesture. Grant then points to the laundry house on the left hand side, and Samantha makes a quick left to enter the parking lot.

The rough left turn that Samantha makes shakes both Sam and Grant back and forth. It mingles the clothes in the back together. Grant's bag has fallen onto Sam's bag. When they come to a complete stop, Samantha apologises to Grant for the hard turn. Grant feels some sharp pain in his back, but he tells Samantha that he would be fine and don't worry about it. Grant manages to get himself out of the car and make his way into the laundry house to retrieve a basket for their clothes. Samantha gets herself out of the car and begins to stuff the mingled clothes back where they belong. It is a pair of silk white underwear that were died pink. They confused Samantha. She did remember ruining some of Jake's good clothes last month, so she put those dyed underwear in her bag.

As soon as Grant came out with the carts for the clothes, Samantha's phone begins to ring. The call was coming from Jake. She places her hand to her mouth and tells Grant to hush as she takes the call.

"Hello, Jake."

"Hey, babe, how are you?"

"I'm good just doing a little washing right now."

"Oh, really?" Jake says in a playful voice. "Can you run upstairs and grab my gym bag out of the closet and wash those clothes in there?"

"I'm not using the washer at the house. I'm at some wash house."

"Why didn't you use the new washer and dryer combo we just bought? All this time, you tell me to replace the old ugly washer, now you have something state of the art, and you choose to take my expensive clothes to a public wash house?"

"Oh, get over it Jake. The washer is too new for me. I don't have time to hook it up or push buttons I don't understand, or read a manual. I will use it but today is not the day."

Jake looks as if he is puzzled by what Sam tells him. He says to himself, All she had to do is plug it in. He snaps himself out of self-thought and says to Sam, "Okay, never mind about the gym bag. Things are going great out here! The first show is this coming Tuesday. I should be out in Cali before then."

"Okay, that sounds good, Jake."

"Yes, it is. Hey, how is my boy Grant doing these days, you heard from him yet?"

Samantha turns and looks at Grant. Grant senses that his name is now brought up into the conversation, so he stops putting the clothes in the basket, and starts to listen to Sam speak. "Well … he was in an accident!"

"Gosh, is he okay?"

"Yes, Jake, he's fine, although he declined back surgery at this moment, he is fine."

"Wow … well, when you talk to him tell him I said something inspirational." Right after Jake says that, one of his female dancers interrupts his conversation and says that he is needed on the floor. Jake then began to rush his phone time with Sam.

"Next time we talk babe, I'll get the whole story of Grant from you, but right now, I have to get back to work."

"Okay, I understand, I think."

"Okay, Samantha, I'll talk to you later." Right when Sam uttered, "I love you," she hears a dial tone from Jake's end of the phone. She takes the phone down from her ear and slips it in her purse in a depressing manner. Grant can tell something is not right, but he doesn't want to make her feel as though she has to talk about it, if she doesn't want to.

Sam then looks up at Grant and says, "Okay where were we, how can I help?"

Grant tells her, "You've done enough by getting me here. I can wash my own clothes and I'm pretty sure you can wash yours. You just might have some kinky stuff in that basket of yours that you don't me to see." They both start to laugh as they head into the laundry house.

The day continues to pass by as they are washing. The two of them can't keep from laughing and conversing with one another as they do their laundry. Sam even blurts out during one of her laughing sessions how much fun this part of her day has been. Grant compliments her quote by adding his own. He says to her, "I can't even remember the last time I've done laundry and been this happy while doing it!"

Another hour passes. By this time, they are almost done washing. Grant goes on to help Sam put her clothes in the basket. He picks up a handful of clothes and piles them in. Grant then asks her, "So why don't you just fold your clothes here?" He grabs another handful of clothes and drops them in her basket. Grant doesn't even notice the pink-bleached underwear that she mixed with her clothes earlier. His eyes were locked into hers at the time he picked up the clothes. She tells Grant that she prefers to fold them at home. She feels as though there is too much pressure to get them done at the wash house. She needs peace when she folds. Grant chuckles at her comment. She picks up her basket and heads to the car. Grant follows her out as he wheels his clothes in a laundry cart. They load up Samantha's car and she then begins to make the trip back to Grant's house.

After she helps Grant out of the car and into his house with his washed clothes, she gives him a warm embrace and whispers to him how much fun she had. Before they break apart from their hold, she gently kisses him on the cheek. As they are releasing one another, he drags his arms down the sides of her arms, and then their fingers interlock for one last feel from one another. Samantha then turns and heads out the door. Grant closes the door and lays his head on the wooden surface. He feels some way for Sam, but he isn't sure what that some way is.

A day passes and no communication between Grant and Samantha has taken place. They both do whatever they do that occupies their individual lives for that period of time. Even though they didn't see each other, that doesn't mean that they don't think about each other.

Another day was underway, and Grant is in his kitchen fixing himself some breakfast. As he is cooking, his phone began to ring. Grant began to smile when he notices that it is Samantha calling.

"Hey, Sam!"

Grant says in an excited voice. "I was thinking about you a little bit." Grant stops speaking as he listens more intensely and uncovers the cries of Samantha on the other end of the phone.

"Sam? You okay? Talk to me. What's wrong?"

Samantha's silence continues for a while as she sits on the phone with Grant.

Grant continues to try to get Sam to share with him her worries, but she remains quiet still. Very shortly after, Grant says to Samantha, "Whatever it is that has you upset must be something that you cannot overcome by yourself. I guess that's why you called me. I won't let you down, Sam. I'm going to sit right here with you quietly until the crying stops, and your heart flows" Then Grant too becomes silent.

A minute later, Samantha lets out a low toned giggle. Grant hears this throughout her cries. Samantha says "You're so sweet, Grant. That woman must have been a fool to leave you."

"I can't put all the blame on her, Samantha I've had my share of foolishness too.

"It's just that I was willing to work it out. I guess that part was not in her plans."

"Jake calls me last night Grant. I hate it when he calls me all stressed out over work." Samantha begins to cry again. "He really knows how to get to me when he's overworked."

"So what did he say? Did he go into confession mode or something?"

"No, I wish. He just doesn't know how to separate work and home. He mixes them both together and lets me have it. Sometimes I feel as though I can't do anything right. I fly back from NY to Cali on a monthly basis. Then I maintain order in the studio, I handle financial records and I still have to be the wife that Jake dreams of. In all honesty, Grant I don't even know what grade I would give myself." Grant sits on the other end of the phone, still in silence from what he just hears. Samantha begins to speak again.

"I apologize, Grant, maybe I dumped too much on you today. I hope my gloomy day hasn't got you feeling down too."

"No, I'm good Sam. I just wish there was something I could say or do that could possibly make you feel better."

"Just take care of yourself. Give yourself plenty of rest. Start a hobby or something that comforts your soul. Teach yourself how to relax."

Samantha takes a deep breath and then says, "You have an excellent point. For some strange reason, when I was a child, growing my Che-a-pet calmed me down.

Grant responds back and says, "Do they even make those anymore?"

Samantha starts to laugh. "No, silly, maybe I can unleash my green thumb that lays dormant inside of me. I've always thought I could be a great gardener!" Sam says that in a cheerful voice.

"That's great to hear. Then I'm going to send you some seeds of my favorite veggie. You can grow it for me, then come over and cook them for me." They both begin to laugh.

"Grant, like I said earlier, this woman had to be on some weird drug to have let you slip away. Thanks for everything."

"You're welcome, Samantha. Let's just pray that Jake doesn't get a hold of that drug and start using them." Samantha begins to chuckle. They both say goodbye and end the conversation. Right after they hang up their phones, Grant searches for a flower shop to place an order.

Samantha arrives to work a little bit more cheerful on Friday. When she passes up her dancers, they were staring at her with smiles and giggles. Samantha doesn't pay it no attention, she just continues to her office.

Upon arriving at her office, she suddenly stops in the doorway. She stares wide eyed at her desk. Sitting there on top of her desk was a beautiful champagne vase with artistic designs covering it from top to bottom. Inside this vase is a single red rose. It was sitting perfectly in the middle of the other flowers to give it that over the top, romantic look. Leaning up against the vase is a card in an envelope. Samantha walks toward the card. She takes it out of the envelope and begans to read it. The card reads:

> I know I said I was going to send you seeds, but those would have taken too long to become like this rose. I then decided to send you something that represents beauty and strong growth in my life. That is what this rose means to me. You are the rose in my eyes. Now, if you were to pair this rose with yourself, that combined would make the perfect pair of flowers in your office.
>
> Love,
> Grant

After Sam reads this card, she immediately begans to cry. She places the card back up against the vase, leaves her office, and locks the door. On her way out of the building, Sam says to Vickki to continue teaching the class what they did yesterday. Vickki agrees, and Sam was on her way to Grant's house.

It doesn't take Samantha too long to reach Grant's house. On the way there, she bombards herself with questions and anxious thoughts. She doesn't want to come on to Grant the wrong way, but she does want to let him know that she appreciates his heart and his kind words. When she does arrive, she exists her car and began to walk to his door. Samantha hesitates for just a minute, and then she snaps herself out of her state of numbness and rings the doorbell. It takes a while before Grant reaches the front door, but while he was approaching it, he thought to himself, "I'm not expecting no one over today."

Grant opens the door and is very surprised to see Samantha on the other end. Right away, she gives him a strong embrace, cupling her hands within each other behind his back. She lays her head on his chest and sobs tears of joy. She constantly repeats herself over and over, "Thank you, Grant, thank you so much! These flowers and that wonderful card really makes me feel special." Samantha slowly begins to separate herself from Grant. While Grant is still in shock, Samantha says to him, "What are you doing right now?"

"Well, I was getting ready to rehabilitate myself with some tae-bo. I don't know how much I was going to participate in, I was going to at least do one kick and two punches." Samantha starts to laugh uncontrollably. She then says, "Okay…there's been a C.O.P., c'mon lets go." Grant looks at her with confusion written all over his face.

"C.O.P.?"

"Yes, C.O.P—**C**hange **O**f **P**lans. You've shown me that you care, now it's time for me to return the favor." Grant says, "But look how I'm dressed, if I step outside my house people are going to start handing me money." Sam giggles. "C'mon Grant, you look marvelous," Sam says sarcastically. She grabs Grant's hands and leads him out of the house. Grant then begins to follow suit and go along. He locks up his house, and they both walk to her car.

Samantha doesn't quite know what to do for the day, but she knows that she wants to show Grant a good time. Everything she will do today will be spontaneous. The first thing that comes to her mind would be to start off the day with food. She decides to take him to eat.

As they are eating, they engage in a lot of conversation. The subjects range from, sports, politics, high school crushes and all the way up to celebrity crushes. There is loud laughter and snickering heard throughout the restaurant. Admix in the conversation, Grant brings up the fact that he hasn't really traveled through California the way that he would've liked to. By the look on Samantha's face, she was in disbelief by this confession.

"So where is it Grant that you would like to go?"

Grant pauses for a minute and ponders on his choices. He places his hand on his chin and then throws out a couple of places.

"Now, I can say that the scenery is beautiful. I have also been to Palm Desert because that is on the way to the casinos."

Sam begins to laugh and says, "You are just naming some of the places you've been to, I'm trying to extract places in California that you haven't visited yet."

Grant begins to think. All of a sudden, he snaps his fingers in excitement. "Got it! Alcatraz! The city where Alcatraz is located."

"Do you mean San Francisco?"

"Yes, that's exactly what I mean."

Sam chuckles and says, "It's a great place to visit. It's very hilly up that far north. How far north have you been?"

"You really like to have me think way back in my life, huh?" Grant says with a smirk on his face. "The farthest I have been was in Ventura." With another astounded look on Samantha's face she now takes a pause. She checks her watch for the time and she pulls out money for the bill, and leaves it on the table.

Now, Grant is staring at Samantha with an inquisitive expression. "What are you thinking about?"

"I know exactly where we are going next Grant!"

"So you think you're kidnapping me now, Sam?" Sam laughs and says, "No, it's only kidnapping if it's by unlawful force or against one's own will. You are about to freely walk with me to my vehicle and travel with me." Now Grant is even more curious. "Where do you have in mind?"

"I'm taking you to Santa Barbara, Grant. Unless you feel threatened or forced to go with me."

"Absolutely, not ..." Grant says joyfully. "This trip I would like to go on." They both begin to laugh as they approach the exit doors of the restaurant. They get in the car and head up to Santa Barbara.

Hours have gone by, and they have a wonderful time in Santa Barbara. They do a little shopping, a lot of eating and more bonding as the evening progresses. On the way back to L.A., Grant is talking about how refreshing the trip is, and how loose the massages made him feel. He starts to kid around with Sam, telling her that he feels like a younger man.

On the car radio, the advertisement of the Clippers game comes on. Grant immediately says "Blake Griffin, right now, he can't even stop me. I could go one on one with him and blow him out!" Samantha starts to laugh hysterically.

"I know you didn't just challenge Blake Griffin to a one-on-one match!" Samantha looks at her clock in the car and says, "Good! We still have time."

"Time for what, Sam?"

"Well, I think if you want to take him one on one, you should at least see him play first."

"We're going to that Clippers' home game tonight?" Grant's eyes open wide and he says, "You'll never get tickets, and we still have sixty miles until we reach L.A." Samantha turns to Grant, looks him in the eyes and says, "Number 1 rule, never doubt me and my driving. Number 2 rule, never doubt the power of a woman, especially, this woman's power!"

Now Grant is the one who is laughing. "Okay Samantha, whatever you say." Grant says with a big smile on his face.

They arrive at the Staple Center fifteen minutes after the game had begun. Samantha half-parks her car in the parking structure and pays the parking fee. Once again, Samantha proves Grant wrong by scoring two tickets in the mid-section area. She pays a hefty price for them, but nevertheless, she gets them. As they take their seats, Grant is hyped up from the game. He orders their first beer and keep them coming throughout the game.

The closer the game stays, the more excited they became. During the closing minute of the fourth quarter, Grant is on pins and needles. He is out of his seat and can't take his eyes off the final play. This is an intense moment for Sam too as she gulps down another beer. The game ends in a heartbreaker. Blake Griffin misses the last shot to tie the game, and Milwaukee Bucks won. Grant jumps up and down in disbelief and says to Samantha in a "buzzed state of mind" "I'm definitely ready for my one on one now!" He turns to the court and shouts out to Blake, "Hey, buddy. Let's Go! You and me one-on-one! I'll bring the balls!" Samantha laughs at his remarks and pushes him toward the aisles so they could leave.

As they walk toward the car in the parking structure, they both realize that neither of them are capable of driving. Grant turns to Sam and says "So … what plans do you have for tomorrow?"

She says, "Uhm, none really."

"Well, here is a list of options: #1 you can attempt to drive us home. We crash we burn and take innocent people with us, or #2 we catch a taxi to our individual places, and the last#3 we catch a taxi to my place. You can stay there until the morning, since I live the closest to The Staple Center. You could just catch a cab up here tomorrow and get your car."

Samantha looks at Grant with a cute smirk on her face and says, "So those are my options, huh? Guess I have to choose between the last two." Grant smiles a little, and then he looks up a taxi cab company on his phone.

The taxi cab pulls up in front of Grant's house and stops. He turns to Grant in the backseat and nudges his knee, hey buddy, you guys are here." Grant wakes up, which in turn startles Samantha as she was sleeping on Grant's chest. Grant steps out of the taxi and gives the cab driver money for the fare. At this time, Samantha lays her head on the window of the taxi and stares out into the darkness. After Grant explains the directions to the driver, he goes to the back window and signals for Samantha to roll the window down. He tells her how much fun he had, and gives her a kiss on the forehead. He then whispers in her ear, "Have a good night." Grant steps away from the taxi and starts to walk towards his house.

Once inside his house, he goes into the restroom. Grant suddenly hears his doorbell ringing. He is very leery of this ringing of his doorbell at this time of night. He yells out, "Who is it!" and then he checks the peephole. He sees through the peephole that the taxi just pulled off, so he opens his door with his heart beating fast, and his face was overcome with joy as he sees Samantha standing there. She says to him,

"You gave the driver directions to my house but I didn't want to go there. That wasn't my choice. In the parking structure you said …"

All of a sudden, Grant pulls her in for a deep passionate kiss. Samantha closes the door with her foot as they kiss and caress each other. They begin to walk backwards until Grant falls onto the couch. Without missing a beat, Grant rolls off the couch and onto the floor with Samantha. Their lips still locked together, their bodies intermix, and their speech has died down. The only language that is being spoken is through their bodies. Grant thinks to himself, Tonight, is the night I get my revenge.

CHAPTER IX

FEEL MY PAIN

Another day has come. After what seems to have been a twenty-four hour flight for Jake, he finally arrives at L.A.X. He thinks it would be best to rent-a-car. He knows he's not staying here long term. Only the weekend, then he's back to New York. He also figures that it's early, so Samantha may still be at home sleep. Jake goes with his new plan and he rents a car. During the forty-five minute drive home, Jake does not let fatigue get to him. He forces himself to stay awake by listening to the radio and sipping on his coffee. It is now 9:15 am and he heads straight into his house. He leaves his bags in the car.

When Jake walks into the house, he doesn't want to wake Samantha up. He goes into the upstairs restroom and take a shower. He is on a mission to get some sleep after that. With nothing but a towel on Jake tiptoes into his bedroom. He goes into his underwear drawer and grabs a tank top and a pair of boxers. The way that the boxers are folded, he doesn't realize that on the left side was a pink bleach stain. It wasn't until he was putting them on that he recognizes the stain. He says to himself Man, Sam really jacked these up. I hope none of my other clothes are ruined.

Jake pulls the covers back. He is ready to give Samantha a kiss on the forehead as she sleeps, but he is stunned to find only some unfold clothes lying underneath the covers. He goes back to the bathroom to get his cell phone. Jake knows that she isn't at the studio yet, because it doesn't open until noon on Saturday. He calls a few of her friends, but they have no clue where she could be. Jake calls Grant as well, but all he got in-touch with is Grant's answering service, so Jake leaves Grant a message explaining to him to call him as soon as he could. After that message, Jake put on some clothes and heads out the door.

On Jake's quest to find Samantha, he checks her favorite spots to eat, to read, and to walk. He drives pass the studio. When he sees that the lights are all off, and her car is not in the parking lot, he knows she isn't there. The only person who Jake hasn't heard back from at this time is Grant. He picks up his phone and tries Grant again. Seeing that two hours has gone by, Jake figures that Grant would've been up and about by now. He is wrong. Jake hangs up his phone, tosses it in the passenger seat, and heads to his friend's house.

It is now 11:35am. Grant rolls over in his bed and sees Samantha lying next to him. One part of him felt victorious, while the other half felt despicable.

As Samantha still lies in bed, Grant gets up heads for his restroom. Just when he has finished using the toilet, he hears his doorbell ringing while simultaneously followed with knocking.

Grant thinks to himself, "I wasn't expecting any company.", but nevertheless he heads to the door, passing up the foot of his bed as he leaves the room. The clamorous ringing and knocking has awakened Samantha. She sits up in the bed in a disoriented state of mind. It takes her a second to remember where she is at, and what she has done. She places her hand on her forehead and massages her temples as the ringing continues. She yells out, "Grant can you answer the freaking door already!" Then she plops back into bed and places one of the pillows over her head.

She then abruptly sits up and checks for the time. She notices that it is after 11:30am and she hops out of the bed to get her phone, so she can call Vickki. After she explains to Vickki that she will be late, she goes into the restroom to get ready.

Meanwhile, Grant makes it to the door. The ringing of the doorbell is so loud, that the visitor doesn't even hear him asking "who is it". As Grant starts to unlock the door, he twists the doorknob and the ringing stops. Once again, Grant asks, "Who is it?"

"It's me Grant, Jake."

At that moment, Grant eyes open fully. He feels his heart beat racing as though his biggest nightmare is on the other side of the door waiting to be let in. He doesn't know what to say, or how to respond. Just as Grant is about to stop twisting the door knob and lock the door back, Jake has already taken hold of the knob and gently pushes it open. Grant doesn't want to object to Jake coming in because he doesn't want Jake to grow suspicious of his actions.

Jake asks Grant "Hey buddy, how have you been?" He gives Grant a friendly handshake and continues to say, "It's been a while since I've seen you. Sam said you got into an accident."

"Yea, I did. I kinda tweaked my back a little, but I'll make it. It's been a while since I've seen you." Grant nervously responds hoping that Samantha is still asleep.

"So, Grant when is the last time you spoke to Samantha?" I've been looking for her for over two hours." Grant scratches his head, then takes a glance at his closed bedroom door. He says to Jake, "Uhm, she told me she was going to have a late start at the office today. Did you check there?"

"When did she tell you this?"

"Yesterday Jake, we briefly spoke before I did my back rehab."

"Oh, okay, let me head down to the studio now it should be open. If not, something is wrong. Do you want to ride with me Grant?" Grant pauses for a second and says, "Nah, I just woke up. I smell, I'm not dressed, and I'd only slow you down if you wait for me."

After Grant says this he hears his bathroom toilet flush. Apparently Jake hears it too. Silence grows between the two of them as they listen to movement in the room. Grant is becoming very nervous and forcing his brain to think overtime in case she decides to come out the room.

Jake nudges Grant and says, "So that's why you don't want to come with your buddy to the studio." Grant chuckles a little. He then hears his bedroom doorknob turn, having to think quickly, Grant yells out, "Hey babe, my friend Jake is here. Now, if you still want me to keep my end of the bet in the living room, it's not just going to be us two anymore. There will be a third party involved."

When Sam hears this, she frantically slams the door. She picks her shirt up and places it over her mouth to muffle her voice."

"It's okay, Grant, I can wait. We got aaallll day!"

Jake looks Grant eye to eye for a second. He then says, "Back rehab huh?" Then he laughs. "Okay Grant, I'll let you have your fun. I have to go and find my wife. After you have your "rehab", get dressed come down to the studio so we can chill" Grant agrees. Jake walks out of the front door and closes it.

The closer Jake gets to his car, the calmer Grant becomes. Then he yells to Samantha "Hey, you okay in there?" you can come out now." Samantha swings the door open with force. She storms out of the room and walks up to Grant. She stands about three feet from Grant and goes on a rant.

"ARE YOU FREAKING INSANE!!! Why would you EVEN LET HIM IN? What if I didn't catch on to your gesture? That was a bone head move, totally bone head."

"Calm down Sam, first off, like I was supposed to knew that it was Jake, secondly, he opened the door as soon as I unlocked it. What was I supposed to do, not let him in!? That would have been more suspicious than anything. Look, he's gone now, can we just move on to the next phase of our day please." Samantha gets a little closer to Grant. She looks past him and out of the window and notices that his car is still outside.

"I thought you said he was gone."

Now Grant takes a look out of the window. He sees Jake sitting down in his car on the phone. Samantha says, "So did he tell you where he was going?

"Yeah, he's going to find you, and his first stop is the office." Samantha starts to think. She puts her hand over her mouth and yells, "Crap not the office!" she removes her hand from her mouth.

"What's wrong with the office, even if he beats you there, you just come up with another excuse?"

She shakes her head and tells Grant, "It's not that easy. You have to distract him. I have to beat him there.

"Why, what's the rush Sam?

"The flowers you sent me are on my desk with the card! My office is locked, but he has the key."

Now Grant begins to pace. They both hear Jake's car start up. Immediately, they look at each other. Samantha says to Grant in a stern voice, "Stall him."

Grant responds by telling Sam to call Jake in fifteen minutes to tell him she is not going to be at the office for another hour. Samantha then runs to Grant's room as Grant bolts out of the front door to flag down Jake.

With minor back pain, Grant waves his arms and runs toward Jake's car. Before Jake pulls off, he notices Grant in the corner of his eye. He puts the vehicle back into park and rolls down the window.

"I thought you had left already. If the offer for me to roll with you is still good I'll take you up on it."

Jake says, "Yeah, you can still roll with me."

"GREAT! Let me just grab my jacket." Jake agrees and Grant goes to retrieve his jacket. He tells Samantha, "Call in fifteen minutes, don't forget." Samantha agrees and continues to rush herself dressed.

Grant really doesn't have anything to talk about while riding in the car with Jake. He is still feeling agitated on whether or not Samantha will call in a few minutes like she is supposed to. Jake feels a little uncomfortable with all the silence, so he decides to spark up a conversation.

"When I first heard you were in an accident, I got real scared for you. I was about to buy a ticket to come out here, but Sam gave me the details of your injuries. After she told me that you were okay, I was relieved. I thought to myself, Grant is a big boy. He will be okay. Now, looking back on things, I probably should have still come."

"It's all right Jake. You're right. I am a big boy. It was a scary time for me but I got through it. Just by you telling me this, lets me know that your heart was in the right place."

The car goes silent again, but this time not for long. Jake's cell begins to ring. In a rigid voice, he answers the phone. "Hello! Where the hell are you! I've been looking for you for hours." Grant knows by Jake's greeting that it is Samantha on the phone. He then over hears Samantha snapping back a Jake.

"I'm not a child and you have no right to talk to me like that!" Jake calms down as he slows down the vehicle.

They are now in the parking lot of the Studio. Jake puts the car in park and continues to talk to Sam. Grant steps out of the car at this time and he prays that she gets him to leave from the studio. After about five minutes of conversation, Jake rolls down his window and signals to Grant.

"Hey, she's not even here yet. She said she's at the gym. I really can't go over no reports or anything without her."

"So how long is she expecting us to wait?"

"Maybe an hour."

"Well … that's a long time to be waiting in the parking lot. We don't have to wait here, Grant, we can go inside the studio. Besides I haven't seen it in weeks. I'm paying a lot for something I'm not even occupying." Jake opens his car door. Grant quickly says "You took me to your restaurant, let me take you to one of my favorites, Jake."

"Well, I am hungry."

Jake throws Grant the keys to his car and says okay buddy let's roll.

As soon as Grant drives away from the studio, he feels at ease about the situation.

Meanwhile…

Samantha arrives at the parking structure via cab and settles into her car. She starts the vehicle and heads to the studio to beat Jake there.

Jake and Grant arrive at Denny's. Jake turn's to Grant and says "Denny's? You've got to be kidding me. We drove three miles to this Denny's and it is one in the strip mall across the street from the studio."

"Hey, I said one of my favorite places to eat. I don't go to that Denny's at the strip mall."

They get out of the car and head inside for something to eat. Once inside, they are seated and handed menus. They decline the menus because they already have in mind what they are going to get. They place their orders and the waitress leaves to go and give their selections to the cook.

Out of nowhere, Jake says to Grant, "Do you think Sam is capable of cheating on me?" Grant is in total shock by this question, in part to the fact that he knows the answer. He also knows he can't reveal this answer to Jake. Grant stammers for the right thing to say.

"I … I … well … what do you think? Do you think it's possible?" Jake sits up in his chair and thinks for a while.

"You know with all of my pass transgressions against her, karma would be cold, but right to strike me at this time. I've been in New York for the better part of two months, but I've been faithful. I'm fulfilling my marital obligations through all of the temptations that is before me."

"Okay, Jake so what gives you the feeling that she is cheating?"

"I don't know, I mean she tells me she is at the gym today. I canceled our memberships a month ago. I was going to switch us to twenty-four hour fitness. The way she was talking, she didn't have any problem at all getting access to the gym. Then a week ago, she goes washing. She totally messes up some of my clothes. We have a new washer and dryer set that she could have used. Maybe, I'm just imagining things."

Grant says to Jake "You shouldn't worry too much over the little stuff. You will drive yourself crazy. Trust me. I jumped on that train before, and I almost rode it straight into hell." They both laugh as food is being sat in front of them. Jake says to Grant "I just hope her bleaching frenzy didn't affect any of my shirts. I paid a lot of money on those shirts." Grant starts to laugh all by himself and says "I'm pretty sure she could not have done any worse than me. When Julia first left me, I did my own laundry and wiped out half of my wardrobe with bleach." He is still laughing as he explains the story. "The one thing I regret is ruining my silk boxers. I turned the left side pink. That was the last gift from my ex-wife."

"Did you say here name was Julia?"

Grant realizes that he did say her name. Now he tries to clean it up quickly.

"I don't remember saying her name. She's the one person I don't like to talk about anymore."

"Oh. Okay, I understand."

"I used to know a Julia for a brief minute." To change the subject Grant says to Jake. "I think we have been here long enough. Let's go see if Sam … mantha has made it in yet."

Jake agrees and they start to head for the car. Grant goes on to pay the bill. Now they both head out to the studio to meet Samantha.

When Samantha makes it to the studio, she scans the parking lot to see if she sees Jake's car. It brought her a sigh of relief not to have spotted his car. Samantha gathers her things and briskly heads to the building. Totally unaware of her surroundings, at this time, Jake pulls up in front of her, and cuts off her pathway to the studio.

"Where have you been?" Samantha realizes who it is and starts to feel a little panicked.

"You scared the crap out of me! Why would you just pull up on me like that and stop? What if I decided to start running? You would've run me down!"

"Well the point is you didn't start running and I didn't hit you. So you just answered your own question. You are not dressed like you just came from the gym."

The two of them grew silent. Samantha then turns and looks at Grant who is sitting in the passenger seat. They greet one another. Jake, for some reason, senses a vibe between the two. He doesn't know if he feels good about the vibe, or bad. He just knows that his gut is telling his something. Immediately, Jake asks Grant can he go and park the car. Grant says to Jake "No problem, man."

So now Jake and Samantha walk into the studio in silence. She's praying that in some way, the two of them seperate so she can get rid of the flowers and the card. Samantha tries to engage in a conversation with Jake to ease the tension that has crept up between them.

"So how was your flight to L.A.?"

"My flight? My flight was outstanding. I had snacks, took a wonderful nap, and got a pair of ear phones for free. It was the best flight I have ever had!" Jake says all of this in sarcastic tone. "The trouble began with my landing in L.A. You wasn't there to pick me up." They enter into the studio, and everyone is preoccupied with dancing that Jake & Sam go unnoticed talking by the entrance doors.

"Look, Jake, I'm sorry I forgot you were coming today. I have a lot of stuff on my plate too, you know, at least, your plate only consists of being in New York on a regular basis. Try flying back from Cali to New York multiple times and see what you remember." Samantha turns away from Jake and starts to walk to her office. Jake is feeling bad now. Guilt has stricken his heart at this time, and he starts to run up after Samantha. As Jake is walking, calling out for Samantha, she calling out for Vickki. "Oh, there you go Saman ... " Vickki's eyes open wide as she looks past Samantha and spots Jake. She is super excited to see him. She runs over in their direction and stops to talk to Samantha first. Vickki doesn't want to disrespect Samantha by going straight to Jake. What Vickki didn't know is that is what Samantha wanted to happen. After a very brief conversation, Samantha told Vickki to fill Jake in on the new enrollee's to the studio.

Vickki agrees. She stops Jake before he has a chance to reach Samantha. This sudden encounter between Jake and Vickki is just what Samantha needs to get a few more steps ahead of Jake.

Samantha finally reaches her office door. she unlocks it, and steps inside the office, then she closes the door behind her. She looks around the room for a place to put the flower but nothing seems logical. She grabs the card and hastily put it in her purse. She then picks up the vase of flowers. She opens her office door, and Jake stares into her direction as she holds the vase up at eye level.

"Where did you get those?"

"I don't know they didn't come with a card or anything. I just got in my office. I'm as stumped at you."

Jake walks closer to Samantha. "Let me see those?"

"What exactly do you have in mind to do to these flowers Jake?

"I don't know yet, I want to admire them much like you are doing."

Samantha holds out the vase for Jake to grasp. Jake places both of his hands on the vase and inspects it. He turns it from side to side. He looks at the bottom of the vase, and then he looks at the arrangement of the flowers. Jake says to himself, "It's only one rose in here?" He ponders on what he just said. Then he repeats himself. "It's only one rose?"

Timing could not have not been any better depending on who you are at this moment. Grant knocks on Samantha's open office door. Both Samantha and Jake turn and look at Grant.

"I parked kinda far back. It is a 'Chick-Fillet' grand opening. The line for that place is ridiculous. Hey, anybody in the mood for chicken?" Jake places the vase on Samantha's desk as he replies back to Grant.

"No, thanks man, we just ate." Jake looks at Samantha as he picks up the single rose in that vase and says. "Well, since you are okay. I'm going home to finish my nap. Well, talk about this rose later."

Samantha begins to tear up and says nothing to Jake as he heads out to the door. Grant moves out of the doorway so that Jake can get through.

Once Grant sees him clear the hallway, he whispers to Samantha, "Did he see the card?" with tears running down Samantha's cheeks, she looks at Grant and says one word, "No." She then goes into the restroom to be alone. Grant looks out of Samantha's window and he sees Jake in his car leaving the property. Grant decides to leave as well. He knocks softly on the bathroom door and says to Samantha, "I'm sorry."

Samantha hears her office door close gently. She doesn't bother to come out of the restroom. She stays there for a while to collect her thoughts.

When Jake finally makes it home, he is exhausted from today's events. He walks into his and tosses the rose on the floor. Jake sits on the edge of his bed and starts to think about all of his suspicions. As he thinks, he disrobes, and gets ready to take a nap. First the shirt, then the tank top is removed. The shoes and socks were next to go, and lastly his pants. Jake stands up to take his pants off. He unfastens his belt and pulls them down. He steps out of his pants and kicks them away from the bed, bringing attention to his boxers. He then crawls into his bed and curls up under the covers. Jake closes his eyes and begins to doze off.

His eyes suddenly open wide. He throws the cover off himself and leaps out of bed. Jake looks down at the boxers that he is wearing and realizes that they are not his. He thinks back to the conversation at Denny's he had with Grant. His mind starts to race. He then looks at the rose and remembers his own story of the rose he gave to Julia. He then remembers Grant mentioning his ex-wife's name at Denny's. It's becoming clear to Jake what is going on. The more he thinks, the angrier he becomes. Jake rips off the boxers that he has on. His blood is boiling. He doesn't know what exactly he wants to do about this, but he definitely knows what he has in mind. As Jake is getting dressed, he thinks of one of his friends who can help him out. He grabs his keys and leaves his house, and heads over to pay Jimmy a visit.

CHAPTER X

OPEN YOUR EYES

Today was a day that seems to fly by quickly for everyone involved in its events. As the sun is setting, Grant has not received a text or call from Samantha, nor has he sent any himself. Communications between the three has come to a halt. With this action fresh on Grant's mind, he wonders what did Jake really know about himself and Samantha. Of course Grant doesn't want to bring any light into a dark situation, so he doesn't try to contact Jake either. The one person that Grant does decide to call is Tim. Grant has let no one know of his vindictive plot against Jake, but he really wants someone to talk to at this time. Tim has always been there for Grant. Even in the time that Grant had pushed Tim out of his life, he knew that Tim was the one who could be trusted, and the one friend would listen.

On the second ring, Tim picks up the phone. He began to greet Grant, and fills him in on what's happening with his family. Grant is happy to hear from his friend, and decides to listen to his stories. After a few minutes of talking, Tim interrupts his own dialogue and apologizes to Grant for not shutting up. They chuckle, and Tim finally asks grant how's everything been with him. A second goes by, and Grant says to Tim. "Better days … better days … I have had some better days in my life."

"Hey, buddy, what do you mean by that? You sound depressed and on a ledge. You're not planning to do anything stupid are you?"

"You know me, Tim, 'Stupid' is my middle name. I actually am planning on doing something stupid, but it's not what you think. I would like to live a lot longer than I am currently living." Tim gives a sigh of relief, then he goes on to say, "Okay, so if that's not your dilemma, what is?"

Grant says to Tim. "Well…It's a long story, so I want bore you with minor details. I'll just get straight to the important parts." Grant then tells Tim what's been going on in his life.

Meanwhile…

Not only was the weather a little gritty and cold, so was the feeling of walking toward her house as Samantha steps onto the stairs. She notices from outside of her house that Jake was home. His car is in the driveway, and there are lights on in the house. The closer she gets to the front door, the more she began to tremble. Jake never did have a quiet spirit when angered, but he also was never the violent type. His weapon of choice was always his vocal chords. He uses words and phrases in ways that would cut you just as deeply and as painful as a knife would.

Samantha finally reaches the top step of her home. She begins to stare at the door handle, and slowly pulls out her keys. She takes a deep breath, and says to herself, I can't avoid the inevitable, I will have to see him sooner or later. It's just Jake … It's just Jake. All I have to do is remind myself, that it's only Jake. Samantha pumps herself up to go into the house.

To her surprise when she enters inside it is very quiet, and well organized. Samantha has come all the way into the house and locks the door. She smells a terrific aroma coming from the kitchen. She began to call out for Jake softly as she turns the corner and enters into the kitchen. Jake turns around as he is stirring up the dish on the stove and answers Samantha's call. "Wow, Jake! This food smells real good. What are you making?"

Samantha continues to walk toward Jake as she is speaking. She is almost close enough to give him a soft embrace.

Jake quickly extends the wooden spoon out in front of Samantha, thus keeping them from contacting one another. "Not now, Samantha. I'm cooking." Jake says in a stern voice. He turns back around and continues to prepare the meal. Samantha kinda found that response too cold, but she figures that he is still angry and wants some answers. She also figures that this is his way of getting them. Samantha then turns around and heads to the dining area. She walks into the dining room and sees two plates have been set up on the table. She picks out a place for her to sit and wait for Jake to conduct the rest of the night. She gets back up and hangs her coat inside the closet in the hallway before Jake complains about it lying on the couch.

Samantha sits dormant for at least ten minutes waiting on Jake to walk up into the dining room. She finally decides to take her phone out from her purse and check her e-mails and do other business-related activities. Now that her attention is locked in on the phone, she hasn't realized another ten minutes has gone by.

Jake suddenly taps Samantha on her shoulder and startles her.

"Wow! You scared the bee-Jesus out of me again Jake!" He places Samantha's meal down in front of her, and responds to her comment with a question. "Who are you texting?"

"Texting? I wasn't texting anyone, Jake. I was checking my e-mails. I became very bored and alone in here waiting for you, so I decided to make the best of my time."

Without responding to that comment, Jake walks back into the kitchen, picks up his own plate, and brings it into the dining room. Samantha senses that this is going to be a long dinner so she places her phone back inside her purse and waits for Jake to have a seat at the table.

After Jake has taken his seat, he starts eating. Now, Samantha began to worry. She has never seen Jake act like this in the four years that she has known him. She wants to ask him a question but she just can't allow the words to escape her mouth. Samantha then turns her attention toward the plate of food in front of her and began eating. She lightly picks around her food, because at any moment, she was expecting Jake to ask her a question.

Four minutes into the meal, Jake puts his silverware down and says, "How do you like the food?" Still being in a puzzled state of mind, Samantha was slow to answer. "It's good. I never knew you know …" Jake cuts her off and starts talking right over her. "I guess a man never knows the extent of love he has for a woman until that woman is gone." Now Samantha sit in confusion.

"Why would you say that?"

"Samantha, I know I've messed up a lot in the past. As of recently, as your husband, I've been outstanding."

"Jake, not only are you confusing me. YOU'RE SCARING ME!" Jake continues to talk, disregarding Samantha's statement.

"I've been doing a lot and I mean a lot of thinking. I didn't know you were out for revenge, Samantha."

"Revenge? Jake what are you talking about!" Samantha begins to raise her voice. She is feeling nauseous and getting irate at this point. As she continues to search for clues about Jake's statements, Jake begins to over talk Samantha. Now Jake starts to shout. During this brief shouting match, Jake yells out, "Do you love him!"

The room goes silently. Samantha is not sure that she understands the question, but she answers it any way.

"Yes Jake, I love you. Why would you ask that?"

"I said, do you love him?"

"Who is him, Jake?" Jake becomes filled with anger and says, "GRANT! DO YOU LOVE GRANT!"

Samantha stammers her words, "Thi … this is ridiculous! Whatever you think you know, you don't! Stop it Jake!"

"No, you stop it! Come clean, Samantha, Don't make me DO THIS!"

"Do what, Jake! You're talking foolish talk! I'm leaving!" Samantha stands up and nearly falls forward onto the table. She catches herself and begins to leave the table. Jake continues to sit at the table. He yells for Samantha to have a seat. Samantha ignores his plea.

As she is walking away from the table, she here's a clicking noise coming from Jake's direction. He then yells out, "I'm not asking you to have a seat, I'm telling you!"

Samantha turns around and sees that Jake has a gun pointed right at her. She realizes that the clicking sound was actually Jake loading one bullet into the chamber. Struck with panic, Samantha drops her purse and covers her mouth with both hands. As she looks Jake square in the eyes, she realizes that something in him just snapped. There's no turning back from where he is now. Samantha walks toward the table and begins to sit down. Her eyes fill up with tears and she asks Jake, "Why?" His response to her was, "In due time, you will see." Her vision began to become blurry. She could hardly keep her head up right. She feels her body shutting down but she doesn't know why. Before she passes out, the last thing she seen is Jake reaching inside of her purse and pulling out her phone. Samantha says, "Where did you even get a gun fr ... " she passes out.

Jake tilts her head up and says, "The same place I got the drugs. Remember, I know people."

While Grant is talking to Tim about Samantha, he receives a text from her phone. The text reads. "Hey, Grant, I don't know what to do. Jake claims to know something is going on. He took a cab to the airport and said he'll be back next week to straighten all of this out. Can you come over so we can figure out how we're going to handle this?" Grant is hesitant about responding, but he sends a text telling her he would be there in about an hour.

Grant then tells Tim that he is going to meet up with Samantha.

"You're going tonight?"

"I don't think that's a good idea. At least come and get me so you don't have to go alone."

"Thanks for the concern, Tim, but I'll be fine."

"C'mon Grant. Okay hear me out then. Let me meet you over there. You know anything can happen."

Grant thinks about it and then gives Tim the address. Grant says goodbye and they hang up the phone. He now starts his journey over to Samantha's house. On his way toward the house, he thinks of things to say to her. Grant really considers coming clean to Samantha about his plot for revenge.

He doesn't want this affair to get any deeper than it already has. He is nervous, but yet at the same time he gathers up more strength to tell her the truth. Nothing else ran through Grant's mind during his fifty-minute drive to Samantha's house. He has a hard decision to make this night, and he knows that he has to make the right choice.

When he arrives at his destination, he shuts the car off and sits there for a minute. He checks his watch and takes a deep breath. Grant notices Jake's rental car in the driveway and he becomes troubled. He then remembers Samantha's text saying that he has taken a taxi to the airport. His heart begins to ease up then. Grant steps out of his car and heads for the house. He gets to the doorstep and knocks. He waits for a minute, then he began to knock again and ring the doorbell as well. He looks at a text message and it reads:

"If that's you at the front door come on in, I'm in the restroom and I will be out in a moment."

He looks at his own rental car and thinks about leaving. Grant takes a few steps down, away from the door, then he quickly turns back around and says, "Screw it." He enters Samantha's house. He smells the tasteful aroma of dinner in the air. He notices that the house is quiet. Grant closes the front door.

He walks straight down the hall and glances into the kitchen. No one is in there, but there are pots on and pans full of food on the stove. He continues straight down the hall. He glances upstairs and sees that the bathroom light is on. He continues to walk. He heads for the dining room. Before he is able to see the inside of the dining room, he hears what sounds to be a muffled voice coming from inside that room. Now, concerns for himself and Samantha comes to mind. He wants to leave out of this house, but a part of him just has to investigate to see what's going on.

He continues to walk toward the dining room, more slowly and cautious now. The muffled voice gets louder. Now he hears a thumping noise which grows louder with each footstep he takes. He passes the closet in the hallway and peers inside the ajar dining room door. To his misfortune, he can see nothing. He places his left hand on the dining room door and shoves it all the way open. He goes into total disbelief when he spots Samantha tied up and bound to a chair. She is rocking and screaming, but cannot be understood because of the tape that is covering her mouth. Grant looks her right in the eyes. As he does this, she stares right back into his eyes with a terrified look in her own eyes.

From behind Grant, the closet door swings open, and a gun swiftly bashes him in the back of the head. Then he is forcefully shoved into the direction of the chair Jake was sitting in. Grant goes hurling out of control and becomes entangled with the chair. This hard fall tweaks his back muscles and causes him to succumb to immediate pain. It was almost as though Grant were paralyzed. Before he could turn to face his attacker, he quickly rotates from his stomach onto his back.

Out of the blue, Grant is being bombarded with punches to the face. Some hits occur with the gun, and some with the unarmed hand. Samantha is losing her mind and voice. She feels so helpless. She doesn't want to watch, but she has no choice. Jake has finally calls off his brutal attack on Grant. He eases off Grant and gives him some space. Grant has taken a severe beating from Jake. His left eye is closing up on him. His nose and lips are busted, and his jaw seems to be out of alignment. With Grant's good eye, he sees the man responsible for his painful condition. He turns to the right side of his body, and spit out the blood that is pouring from his mouth. Grant looks up and down at Jake and he sees the weapon that is in Jake's hand.

Jake then starts to take steps toward Samantha.

"No!" Grant yells. He pivots from his back onto his stomach, and he starts to crawl toward the dining room wall. Weak and severely bruised, this action takes all the strength that Grant has left. Jake allows him crawl to the wall. He knows that in Grant's condition, there is minimal damage he can create. Jake reaches Samantha and rips the tape off her mouth.

The first thing she does is yell out for Grant. This gesture enrages Jake even more. He briskly walks back over into Grant's direction.

"Is this who you want?!" Jake kicks Grant in the back as he is crawling.

This brings Grant to a halt. He falls flat on his stomach. "Samantha, how could you? I love you! I work hard for everything we have! EVERYTHING WE GOT! I gave up my childish ways for you! THIS IS WHAT I GET!"

Grant manages to make it to the wall and puts his back up against it. He sits up and laughs out loud.

"Childish ways, huh? So during your childish outtakes, you didn't think there would be any reparations for your wrongdoing?"

Jake points the gun at Grant and says, "You shut the hell up, Grant, no one is talking to you. No one!"

"Well, I'm talking to you, Jake! I just done to you what you've done to me!"

" … And what is that Grant, huh?"

"I ruined your marriage! Now we're even!"

"Even? Even? You're bruised, beaten, and close to dying. I don't think even is the word."

Grant says "Oh yeah? You think so, just ask Samantha." Grant starts to laugh as he feels the pain of his wounds at the same time.

Jake looks at Samantha, he bares no expression on his face, just a blank hard stare. He starts to walk toward Sam, but turns back around. His attention is set once again on Grant. He walks over to Grant clearing his path of chairs, and broken dishes. He tells Grant, "So you think all of this was worth it? … the re-aggravation of your back pains? The scars from a pistol whipping? The broken ribs from a kick?" Now Jake is standing about five feet from Grant. Jake takes a deep breath and stares into Grant's eyes. From Samantha's point of view, there is no fear in either man's eyes. If she was to sum it all up, there is only going to be one survivor in this finale. Grant starts to speak to Jake.

"You know, after all is said and done, I got what I wanted. Not so much Samantha, but revenge. Us men seem to feed and live off that stuff, Jake. If you don't believe me, just take a look around your dining room."

Jake starts to slowly raise the gun up from his hip. As the gun is being raised, Grant quietly whispers, "I win."

Jake doesn't quite understand what Grant has just said, so he asks him to say it louder. Grant raises his voice and yells. "I WIN, JAKE! I WIN!"

By this time, Tim's car pulls up outside of Jake's place. He quickly gets out of his car and sees that Grant's rental car is still there. As Tim walks closer to the front door, he hears yelling coming from the house. He takes out his phone and calls the police. While Tim is still on the line with emergency dispatch, he rushes to the front door.

Jake is telling Grant over and over again to shut up. Grant is just holding his ground and continuing to speak. He even throws in a laugh from time to time. Jake is highly upset that Grant will not shut up. He is upset that Grant finds something so funny, and he is upset that he knows there is no turning back from this. Jake says to Grant, "So you want funny, I'll tell you what's funny! Pretending to be my friend, pretending not to want to betray me every single day you saw me … and pretending not to love my wife just to get your revenge!" Grant chimes in and says, "I never loved Samantha the way that I love Julia! I just believed both of them deserved better than YOU!"

Jake turns his back toward Grant and walks away. He utters, "This guy just doesn't know when to SHUT THE HELL UP!"

While Jake's back is facing Grant, he raises the gun up toward Grant and fires off three shots blindly into his direction. Samantha starts screaming from the top of her lungs. Bouncing up and down in the chair, she almost has the restraints loosened, but they are fastened pretty well. Samantha yells Grant's name over and over, but he is reluctant to answer.

Jake drops the gun while facing Samantha and falls to his knees.

"I'm sorry, baby, I'm sorry. He left me with no choice." Jake rests his face in his hands while he sinks to the floor while sobbing.

Tim rushes into the dining room, spots the gun, and picks it up instantly. Jake hasn't noticed that Tim was in there until Tim kicks Jake in his side, that makes him fall upon his back. Tim is still in confusion to what all has taken place. Samantha is screaming, "Help Grant! Help Grant!" and Jake is crying with his hands on his head, while lying on his back. Tim starts to scan the room for Grant.

It isn't until Tim does a 180-degree turn that he discovers Grant. He immediately sees one bullet hole, two feet from Grant's head.

He sees Grant's left foot bleeding with a hole in the bottom of the shoe, and he sees the look on Grant's face as he sits against the wall clutching his stomach. Grant's shirt soaks with blood, and he can't begin to form any words. He is gasping for air.

As the police sirens grow louder, the less time it seems that Grant has to live. Samantha finally breaks the wooden chair that she was restrained to, and runs over to aide Grant. Jake then tries to get up, but Tim continues to point the gun at him, and tells him not to move.

Samantha wraps her arms around Grant. "Everything is going to be okay. You will be fine. Just stay with us … Stay with us." Samantha says these words to Grant as she rocks him back and forth.

The police finally storm the house and order both Jake and Tim on their backs. Samantha yells at the officers "Where's the damn ambulance! Get an ambulance out here! He's dying!" One of the officers radios in for an ambulance.

Grant is taking slow, but very deep breaths, not knowing which one will be his last. He grows numb to the pain that his body is in, because he is now beginning to fade away. Everytime he closes his eyes, he is jolted by Samantha to "Wake up! help is almost here. Just stay a little while longer."

In Grant's mind, he doesn't know how much longer he can hold out. More commotions is brought into the room with the arrival of the emergency response team. They make their way over to Grant, and place the oxygen mask on his face. As he starts to breathe in fresh oxygen, he loses consciousness. As the paramedics lay him on the stretcher and rushes him to the ambulance, Tim pleads his case to the arresting officers. Once inside the ambulance, the paramedics have only minutes to put Grant where he needs to be. Samantha is watching at them operate on Grant before they close the doors and drive away. She know in her heart that this doesn't look good for Grant at all.

She then hops into her car to meet up with him at the hospital. Tim already has headed down that way also, as soon as the police let him leave.

Grant opens his eyes to the sight of bright lights and a lot of people. There is a lot of people, fast talking, big words, and rapid movement going on around him. When Grant tries to lift his head, he is denied that action and told to lie still. He now realizes that he is in the hospital on a gurney. He feels his own hands against his body and notices that they are soaked. He doesn't remember all the details, but he knows he is in trouble.

Through all of the people surrounding his gurney, he is able to make out Tim's face amongst the crowd. Tim could see Grant looking at him, but he encourages Grant not to speak. The next thing that Grant realizes is that he is put into an elevator. Tim tries to make his way in there as well, but he is denied access. Grant sees Tim sink onto the hallway wall as he is relaying Grant's condition to someone on the phone. Before the elevator doors close, Grant hears Tim speak into his phone conversation that if he doesn't have surgery right this instant, he is not going to make it.

When the elevator doors open up, the doctors rush Grant into the operating room. Not long after he was transferred from the gurney to the operating table, he starts to cough up blood and shake violently. Grant's world suddenly becomes dark again.

With Grant now lying flat on his back, he opens his eyes. He looks around and sees no one. He doesn't find it strange. It was a beautiful day, not a cloud in the sky. It looks like it's around eighty-eight degrees outside. A nice day for a walk. He turns his attention away from the window, and glances outside of his room. It might be a chaotic scene, outside of his hospital room but it is as quiet as quiet can get on the inside.

Grant hears his room door handle jiggle and someone walks in. He realizes that it is Tim. He looks as though he misplaced something, and now is trying to find it. He walks around the foot of Grant's bed and says, "Ah, ha! There you go," in a low-toned voice. He bends over and picks up his keys and begins to leave the room. From the corner of Tim's eye, he sees Grant elevating his hand. Tim turns to Grant and gives him face to face contact. He is overcome with joy. Grant smiles heavily and tries to talk. Before Grant could utter a word, Tim says "Wait, wait, don't talk. The doctor said you can have visitors as long as we don't make you speak. You've been in and out for the better part of four days now. You just missed Carol and the kids." Grant tries to form words, but Tim cuts him off again.

"Why are you trying to be a rebel? You will have plenty of time to talk. Everything went well on the surgery table. You're going to be okay." Grant smiles and nods his head up and down.

"Now, Grant, you always know when to wake up at the most inconvenient times. I left my keys up here but I found them. Now I have to go eat with the in-laws, and I'm already late!"

Grant lets out a chuckle. Tim pats Grant on his shoulder, and tells him that he'll be by tomorrow. Grant nods his head in approval. Grant extends his hand for a handshake and Tim honors him with one. Grant watches Tim as he exits the room. Grant starts to feel sleepy once again from all the medicine and he dozes off a few minutes later.

This time Grant is awakened by the sound of the room door closing. He can see the nurse leaving his room direction from looking out of the pane of glass in the hospital door. The room is still quiet, except this time, it has a few changes. The curtains are closed and it is dark outside. The only noise that is being heard is by the machines monitoring his health.

Grant swiftly turns his attention to the left of him and notices a big bouquet of flowers. He says to himself, These weren't here before. He curiously looks at the flowers and wonders who they came from. He then hears someone clear their throat, as they sit in the hospital chair that the big bouquet is blocking. He peers over the flowers, but still can't quite make out who it is. Grant then gently pushes the bouquet to the side to reveal the face of the stranger.

No words could describe what Grant feels to see her sleeping. With her eyes closed, reclining in that hospital chair, with a thin blanket on, she is a delightful view to gaze upon.

Grant tears up instantly and says to himself, "If this is true, if this is really you, I will love you unconditionally. Nothing will shake our foundation. Nothing will weaken our borders. If you are truly here, to love me, to give us another chance, then I will gladly accept your offer. If and only if, I am who you want, my precious beloved Julia, then it is 'I' you shall receive. When you open your eyes I promise, this time, things between us will be different."

THE END

www.ingramcontent.com/pod-product-compliance
Lightning Source LLC
Chambersburg PA
CBHW071154300726

48975CB00004B/1154